DARKER

VI CARTER

CHAPTER ONE

MARIA

The cold steel burns under my palm as I push the double doors open. The click of my heels join the beat of my heart. I'm pushing the boundaries with Damien, but I refuse to be ignored.

"Mrs. Callan."

I suppress a smile as Terry scrambles around the lone counter, trying to stop me with a raised hand.

"Please, Mrs. Callan, just let me tell him you're coming." I glance over my shoulder as he scours the desk in his panic for the phone.

"He's in a meeting." His final attempt to slow me down doesn't work. Nothing can stop me. I won't be ignored.

The area grows smaller—and my heart beats faster—as I push down on the gold handles and enter his office. He's in mid-sentence, talking to three other men who all turn, their eyes take in every inch of me. I hold my pose and let them.

The phone on Damien's desk rings with persistence.

"I'm in a meeting," Damien grinds out the words as he leans back in his chair.

"I need to go shopping." I haven't released the door handle and it's keeping me grounded under his gaze. He's always been easy on the eyes, but as he grew, I found myself appreciating him more and more.

Damien sits forward in his chair. I glance at his other colleagues who haven't taken their eyes off me. Capturing the attention of men I have mastered, from years of understanding that our bodies are the forbidden fruit they seek. They'll never have me, but that doesn't stop me from leading them to believe they could.

The one man I could never entice with my curves, and revealing ways, and too much skin, sits in front of me now with a warning flashing in his green eyes. I read the warning loud and clear, and I have a moment of uncertainty. I raise a brow.

"That's what I pay Andrew for." He doesn't release me from his stare as he cuts off the persistent ring of the phone.

"I know. I'm looking at her." He places the phone back in the receiver.

"Andrew is out sick." I pull in my bottom lip and can see the men shift. So easy.

Damien works a muscle in his jaw and I don't move. I won't be dismissed.

"Shall I go myself?" I sing sweetly and turn on my high black heels. The short leather skirt doesn't leave much to the imagination.

Terry frowns at me as I step into the lobby. The three men from the meeting pass me slowly, each one taking a peek. Curiosity and appreciation burns in their eyes.

"Ready?" Damien walks in front of me and I follow his broad back. He's always been an asshole, but since we married two weeks ago, he's moved so high on the asshole scale that I barely recognize him.

Once I step out of the hotel, I push a pair of large black glasses up on my face. Damien holds the door open, his fingers dance over his phone. His attention solely on his phone and not on me. I climb in with a sense of dis-satisfaction at how this all turned out. I had planned to storm his office and demand for him to take me shopping, only I had expected some kind of reaction. The car dips as he gets in and places his phone in its dock.

"Seatbelt." His one-word sentences have me clipping the belt in with a loud click. If he notices, he doesn't show it as he pulls out onto the main road.

Damien's fingers dance across the phone again until the ring fills the car. I glare out the window, but I'm aware of everything about Damien: his cologne; the space he takes up; the space that's empty between us. Yeah, I hate how aware of him I am.

"Terry, get Andrew on the phone and tell him to get to work. If he doesn't, he's not welcome back."

"Yes, sir." Terry's shaky voice has me glancing at Damien.

He ends the call and glares at me.

"I like Andrew, you won't fire him." I give the command and smile at my husband.

He sneers but the heavy breath holds no humor. "I don't have time today, Maria, so be quick."

Silly, silly Damien. Now I'll make sure I take my sweet time.

We pull into a space near the front of the mall. Damien busies himself with his phone, his fingers moving across the screen again as he removes the keys from the ignition and climbs out.

I unbuckle my belt and get out, fixing my short skirt. I didn't even want to shop. Closing the door, the car bleeps. Damien's talking on the phone, rambling off our location.

A group of young people hang out to the left of the door. They must be in their early twenties. One of the guys with a backwards cap wolf-whistles at me. I give him a smile. I appear older than them in my outfit and high heels.

The whistles cease abruptly and I glance back at the group who all look away. Frowning, I peek at Damien who's on his phone again.

My destination has pink neon signs outside. My lips tug up. If this doesn't get a reaction, I'm all out of ideas.

I pick up my pace and Damien matches it. When I peek at him he's looking around him. Not at me. Never at me.

Entering the store, the dim lights make it a very intimate setting.

"Good morning." I'm greeted when I step in and take off my sunglasses.

"Morning." I sing back in my chirpiest voice. The assistant's eyes jump to the looming figure behind me. Her eyes flash with appreciation. I want to tell her he might look like a rising God—or Devil—but he has a personality that could freeze Hell over. Yep, that cold.

I don't think, but randomly select lingerie. My fingers run across the red lacy material as I check the size.

"Can I help you?" The same blonde assistant who greeted us appears.

"That would be fantastic. It's my boyfriend's birthday and I want to wow him."

The blonde's eyes widen. I gaze at her name tag. Elaine.

"Red is his favorite color," I say holding up the red lacy bra.

Elaine gets to work, selecting a red thong, stockings and a black and red suspender belt.

"You can try them on."

My lips tug up higher. "That would be so great." I turn to Damien who looks like he's watching paint dry.

Smiling at Elaine, I take all the goods and follow her to the fitting rooms.

"Oh, I'm sorry sir, you can't be back here." Something in me sings. He followed me, that's what I wanted.

"I'll be right outside." I think his words are for me, but it's hard to tell as he walks out of the fitting room.

"Is he the boyfriend?" Elaine asks as I start to strip.

"No, that's my husband." I push down the skirt with frustration.

"Oh." Elaine's eyebrows rise into her hairline, before she composes herself and draws the curtain around me. Once the world is blocked off I slump down onto the chair. I refuse to meet my eyes in the mirror.

Irritation has me getting into the outfit. I have to get Elaine in to help me clip on the suspender belt. The end result...I would expect to cause a few heads to turn, but there's only one in particular I want to turn. I push back the curtain and move back dangerously close to the opening that leads out onto the floor. From the corner of my eye, his bulking form is there.

"What do you think?" I ask while checking out the back in the mirror. My heart pounds a little faster. I glance at Damien and his eyes skitter across my skin. Goosebumps rise in the wake of his stare.

"It's nice." He turns away with his phone.

Nice? I glance back at myself in the mirror. Nice? I know sexy and this screams sex. Not that I've ever had sex before. My father and brother make sure of that with their overprotective nature.

I pull the curtain around me with more force than necessary and get dressed. I move past Damien quickly as I go to the till and Elaine rings up my purchases. Her eyes keep jumping to Damien. I snort and her cheeks grow red as she focuses on her job. I want to tell her not to bother. He's made of stone. She smiles at him, and when I glance at him, his lip tugs up slightly at her.

Taking my purchases and card from a very distracted assistant, I slap on my glasses and walk as fast as I can in my heels. Damien manages to move beside me like I'm not speed walking in heels. His phone rings and he answers the device that consumes nearly all his attention. Maybe he should have married his phone.

I exhale as the car bleeps and I climb in. I could demand to go somewhere else. Does it matter? Two weeks of this bullshit and yet he avoids me like he got a raw deal.

When my father told me if I didn't marry Damien I wouldn't get my inheritance, I honestly wasn't that outraged. Arranged marriage isn't my thing, but Damien has always caught my attention—and I had thought I'd shown up on his radar a few times.

"I have to get back to the office. I'll drop you off at the house. Nate will be there."

I stare out the window and don't answer Damien. He doesn't seem to care as he drives me back to my gilded cage. My stomach twists and a scream pushes its way up my throat. I squash it as the gates open and we roam up the winding driveway to our marital home. Gifted by my father. The car stops at the main door and Nate appears. The engine still hums.

I glance at Damien and he's watching me. Green eyes consume me and I'm drowning. How easily he can strip me with one glance.

"I have to go, Maria."

I blink and he looks away. Grabbing my shopping bag, I get out of the car. The door clicks behind me and the car tears down the driveway.

"Hello, Princess." Nate greets me.

I take off my sunglasses.

"What's with the long face?"

I'll never tell anyone about how I feel. "Nothing, just Damien pissing me off as usual," I say as we enter the house. Kicking off my heels, I leave them, and my shopping bag, on the floor.

"Could you not find a top in your size?" I tease. Nate's white muscle top is painted onto his hard chest like a second skin.

"I'm your eye candy. I do this for you."

I grin at him. "I'm more of a suit kind of girl." I'm more of a Damien kind of girl.

Everyone in this house knows our marriage was arranged. At first it didn't bother me. But with each dismissal it becomes more painful to be rejected by him.

"You want a drink?" Nate calls as I take the steps up the stairs two at a time.

"Yeah, a Diet Coke." I call over the banister and climb to the first floor. Opening the doors to the master bedroom, I don't look at the unused bed. Flicking on the light, the closet space is illuminated. I shimmy into the black jeans before pulling on a hoodie. Today is a write-off. Swiping my hair up into a bun, I make my way back downstairs.

Nate smiles at me as I enter the kitchen. The tiles are cold under my bare feet. The can is colder as I wrap my fingers around it.

"I see you were shopping." Nate raises an eyebrow.

I shrug. "Yeah, I needed some stuff."

He could look in the bag and call me out on my lie, but Nate doesn't. Instead, he follows me into the living area. I fall back onto the couch and Nate joins me. I'm very aware of how close he sits and how our thighs touch. I can flirt and tease men, but having contact with them, I haven't experienced before. My brain misfires signals telling me Nate's closeness is calculated.

"I would have taken you shopping." I glance at him. His soft brown eyes travel across my face.

I frown. "It's fine, my husband did." I take a sip and allow my words to sink in. Nate still smiles and I know my brain has definitely misfired the signals to me.

"Aren't you sick of babysitting me?" I lean back on the couch and stare at the ceiling.

"No."

Men and their one-word answers. I get off the couch.

"Where are you going?"

"Where can I go?" I fire back.

"Wherever you want, Maria."

I glance at Nate and frown again. "No, I can't." He knew I couldn't go anywhere without someone watching over me. I knew my life before Damien had been overseen by my father, and that had been suffocating. With Damien, it felt worse. He was never here, yet someone else always was. At least with my father, I had him or my brother.

"Where do you want to go?" Nate asks.

"Rome." I fire out randomly. I don't want to see Rome, but I also want to drive my point home.

"Let me see what I can do." Nate's confidence has me laughing as I climb the stairs.

Not a chance.

CHAPTER TWO

DAMIEN

"**M**r. Callan." Terry greets me with hunkered shoulders. "I tried to stop her."

I hold up my hand, cutting off his excuses. I don't look away from him as I gather mail from the desk. "Next time, try harder."

Terry nods and I take the post with me back to my office. Another morning wasted.

The phone rings and I pick it up, cutting off the noise abruptly.

"She wants to go to Rome." Nate's voice carries a smile. He's too fond of Maria for his own good.

"No." I'm ready to hang up.

"What if I go with her?"

I pause in opening the mail. Nate isn't someone I want around my wife. Our arranged marriage doesn't make her any less my property. She comes with a warning label written by her father. I must honor her and protect her until her father decides we can go our separate ways. She is not to be touched—and I can't touch any other woman—while his daughter is under my roof.

"No." I repeat.

"She's not happy." His smile melts into his words.

Taking Maria to Rome would require a lot of security. She has no idea the danger she's in, and her father wants it kept that way. She is his most treasured jewel. He has placed her in my hands because I can protect her and he knows it. Kane knows one side of me, the other I keep hidden from the world—it's the side that I need to keep away from Maria.

"Where is she now?" The image of her standing in the lingerie is seared into my mind. She knows her worth in gold. Each moment being around Maria is a moment too close to me losing all control.

"Upstairs." The crunch of an apple has me growing irritated with Nate.

I hang up as someone knocks on my office door.

"King." I grin as he steps into my office.

"How is my brother?" King has a face that makes women fall at his feet, but a sharpness that makes them run.

"I'm not your brother," I say as he closes the door behind him. I've always respected King, he will take over from his father one day. He is also Maria's brother. Overprotective to the point that I never spoke to her through all the years I've worked for the Andersons. She's always been forbidden and off limits.

"How is my sister?" The question is laced with lairs.

I lean back in my chair. "Going to Rome soon."

King's grin slips. "Are you sure that is wise?"

"Would you like me to tell her no?"

The grin returns. "Take her and as many men as you need."

I wish I would have had all these men at my disposal before. But that's one of the perks to marrying Maria. I get the room to build up my own business, too.

"How is she?" He sits down, crossing a leg over the other. A scar tugs at the right side of his lip.

"Good." Two weeks down and this is a daily thing with King. He always starts off with the intense brother conversation. I don't believe he really thinks he's intimidating me, but I'll play along with his game.

"Me and the boys are having a card game over at Gerald's, you coming?" King's morals shatter now. He knows what he is asking and I know I could take him up on his offer, but it's his father who paid me, not him.

"I'll pass. I have a trip to Rome to organize." Gerald's club is a sex club that I did security for. I don't have to anymore—I'm building up my own security company—but the darker side of me always calls to that place. A side I needed to keep hidden—even from King.

"Lenny said the meeting didn't last long this morning."

I sit forward and shuffle the post. "Maria needed to do some shopping."

I don't meet King's laughing eyes. He exhales loudly and gets out of the chair.

"Is she at home?" He could ring her or just go to our home. He did this to flex his power and we both knew it.

"Yes, she's with Nate."

His smile widens. "Right, brother, I'll see you tonight."

He has my attention now. Tonight? I wasn't aware of any meeting tonight. At my blank expression, he shakes his head. King's demeanor could be mistaken for friendly, but I know better.

"The charity dinner tonight. Father expects you and Maria to be present."

Shit.

"We will be there." Maria must have received the invite and never told me. For all the attention she sought, she didn't actually like the spotlight. In the past, when I did security at these functions, she always looked miserable and would try to blend in, but with Maria that just isn't possible. She holds any room she's in hostage—and only releases them when she leaves.

I stay in the office for the rest of the day and try to burn as much time as I can before I have to go home. Sitting outside the gates, I check my armor for kinks. She'll test me. I don't believe Maria wants me for one second. She's pushing boundaries with her father. Angry at this marriage.

The gates open and I drive slowly up the drive. I don't park the car in the garage, but leave it at the door. In a few hours we will be leaving again.

King's car isn't around and that's one less thing to piss me off. When he's here with his sister she really up's the ante on me.

"You're late again." My greeting from Maria when I step into the foyer. She's changed out of her earlier clothes. I'm grateful that I don't have to fight with myself to not look at her legs, but she still draws my eyes.

"I was busy." I check my phone for any updates. Terry has forwarded me the email for our flights to Rome. First class for six of us.

"I want you here at six from now on." I glance up at Maria, her demands are growing longer every day. Under them, I can sense her irritation. Her brown eyes swirl with anger.

"Hmm." I leave it at that and walk away.

"I won't be ignored." Her words follow me, along with her, into the kitchen. Nate's sitting on the counter.

"Get off the counter."

He slides down at my words.

"Go home." I add and he widens his eyes before leaving the kitchen. He mumbles a goodbye to Maria. I pour myself a coffee and glance at the food on the table. I walk past it and Maria is on my heels.

"I want to go to Rome."

I sip my coffee. "Have your bags ready for the morning."

I glance at her over the rim of my cup.

I expected a smile.

She narrows her eyes, her hand going to her curvy hip. "Really?"

"Have I ever lied to you before?" I take another sip.

Her hand slips from her hip. Conflict has her looking away. "I made you a sandwich."

She's looking for a fight. What a shame she won't be getting one from me.

I go upstairs and she doesn't follow me. It's something I notice about her, she will follow me around downstairs pouring out her demands, and stamping her feet, but never upstairs.

I enter my bedroom and leave my coffee on the bedside table as I strip out of my suit. I don't have to be careful about revealing my back. The crisscross scars aren't sore anymore, but no matter how many times I see them in the mirror, I feel the pain of each lash. I can almost hear the rain drip off the thin roof, some of it falling into the empty tin bucket beside my head. Going into the bathroom, I step into the shower and wash away the memory.

I'm dressed in a tux when I arrive downstairs. She's not around and I pick up the sandwich and eat it as I make myself another coffee.

Checking the time, we have an hour before we have to leave for the charity dinner.

I finish the sandwich and make my way to the sitting room. I pause in the hall. I can hear her moving around upstairs. The slam of a door has me waiting a bit longer until she starts moving around again. She'll be extra fiery tonight. This is our first appearance as a married couple. My stomach tightens as I enter the sitting room. To distract myself, I turn on the TV and watch the hurling.

After another forty minutes, I get up and knock off the TV. She's cutting it tight.

I'm ready to go upstairs when the front door opens. Andrew's eyes meet mine and I move toward the table in the hall. My hand slips under the wood as my eyes stay trained on the door.

Andrew's fingers grow redder as blood pours out of the wound in his stomach.

"Are they still here?" I ask him as I remove the gun from its holder.

He shakes his head while slipping to the floor and I'm beside him. Ducking the gun into my waistband I remove my jacket.

"Keep it on the wound," I say. His face is pale and sweaty. Getting up, I ring Nate as I race up the stairs.

"Maria." I call her name as Nate answers the phone.

"Get over here. Andrew's been stabbed." I hang up as I enter Maria's bedroom, but it's empty. A hollow feeling starts in my stomach and grows as I check her bedroom. She isn't here.

"Maria." I shout her name again and she appears out of my bedroom in a full length black fitted dress. I want to ask her what she was doing in my room, but now isn't the time. Her eyes widen as I reach in and grab her arm. Taking out the phone, I ring King.

"Where are you?" He greets me.

"Andrew is injured, someone's been at the house." Maria's quick inhale has me looking at her. Brown eyes grow wide and her painted red lips part slightly. I steer her into an empty room at the back of the house.

"Maria?" He's moving.

"She's in the safe room now." She glances around the empty space and when I release her and walk away, she's following me. I don't pause as I pull the bullet proof door behind me locking her in.

"Shit."

Andrew has slumped fully across the floor, his eyes closed.

"What's wrong?" King's moving as he speaks.

"It's Andrew." I move the phone to my other ear.

"I'll be there soon." King hangs up the phone and I push the device into my pocket before checking Andrew's pulse. There is a flicker of life. I can't leave the house. The front door is still slightly ajar and I leave it like that so I can see out. Lights flood the driveway as Nate's jeep pulls up outside the house.

"Drop him off at a hospital." I direct.

Nate helps me lift him into the back of the jeep. Andrew groans.

"Andrew, stay with us."

He groans again as I step away and close the door. Nate jumps into the driver's side and leaves. Each shadow could be a potential attacker. Kane has a lot of enemies and so do I. Returning to the house, I search each room to make sure no one has entered.

The front door opens and I swing around with a raised gun. King doesn't flinch at the gun. He closes the door behind him.

I lower the gun and tuck it into my waistband.

"I've two men checking the area. Where is Maria?"

I jut out my chin towards the stairs and he moves up them quickly as I answer my buzzing phone.

"He's dead." Nate tells me the moment I answer the phone.

Shit.

CHAPTER THREE

MARIA

My arm burns from where Damien touched me. I glance around the empty space and all I can think of is why didn't I know we had a safe room? Why do we have a safe room? My heart dances and I take a few steps towards the door. My whole life reminds me of the house of mirrors at a funfair—I never understand what's going on. I'm put in corners and shadows and told to stay put. I've learned over time not to question things.

The door opens and I'm ready to fire a million questions at Damien, but King appears in a tux. His gaze bounces around the room before it lands on me.

His lips tug up. "Sis. You okay?"

"No. I'm not. What's going on?"

His smirk turns into a smile. "Bad form?" He opens the door fully and Damien passes the room.

Hell no.

"What's going on?" I know my brother won't answer me. But my husband should.

His large hands work on the tie around his neck. I notice the speck of blood before he stuffs it into his pocket. "Who's blood is that? Why did you shove me into that room?" My breathing is labored and I sense King behind me smirking. This isn't funny. For once I want to know what is going on. Damien brings out a rebellious side in me that demands answers and wants to be heard.

"Nothing. Let me grab my jacket and we'll go." He pauses at his bedroom door and he glances back at me over his broad shoulder. I see the question there. What had I been doing in his room? I don't want to answer that, so I spin around and fix King with a glare. His smirk lessens, but I can't scare him.

"Damien's right. It was nothing. He thought he heard something. Old age."

It's hard not to smile with King. He's always joking. Life is one big party to him, but he makes me forget the ugly part of life.

"Why don't I believe you?" I ask, as we make our way downstairs.

I reach the hallway first and turn as King clears the last two steps. "I'm not a little girl anymore." My voice has lowered and I feel nervous getting real with King. It isn't something we do. We're so close, but not about things that really matter.

"You will always be my little sister." He throws his arm around my shoulder. "Stop worrying. Tonight, we party."

"It's a charity meal. Not a party." I remind him as Damien comes down the stairs while pulling on a black suit jacket. I lower my lids when his eyes clash with mine. King's laughter rings the whole way out the door and into the waiting car.

"Baby girl." My father greets me, pulling me into his side and places a kiss on my head.

"You look a bit thinner." His dark brows drag down over his dark eyes.

"I'm eating fine." This is a constant with him. He kisses me on the other cheek. "You look stunning as always."

"So do you, dad." He's an older version of King, they could pass as brothers.

I smile at my father and something in me relaxes just being around him and my brother again. King pulls out my chair beside him and I sit down with my father beside King. The seat on the other side of me is empty. I glance around the room for Damien. He's nowhere in sight.

He finally arrives as the meal starts, and I smile and nod when I'm meant to. A photographer moves around the table taking photos. Damien is stiff beside me, and once dessert is over I excuse myself from the table. He glances at me and I ignore his eyes that follow me across the room. I need to get away from him. Sitting that close had my stomach squeezing every few seconds. No one has ever made me nervous, but he has that effect on me and I hate it.

"Gin and tonic," I order at the bar. I smile as people meet my eyes from around the room. A charity dinner that costs more than it raised. It's just an excuse for people with money to get together; and I've always hated these parties. Too many people watching. Someone is always watching.

"Marcus."

"Maria." I take the hand of the man to my left. His black hair is peppered with strands of gray. Dark blue eyes smile at me and I know his type: wealthy, single, and always looking for the youngest in the room.

"I haven't taken my eyes off you."

I accept my drink and smile at Marcus. "Is that so?" I take a sip of my gin and tonic slowly.

His gaze jumps to my lips before he returns back to the barman and orders a white wine.

"I've seen you before."

"Have you?" I place my drink on the counter.

"Yes." He doesn't say where and his eyes roam across my black fitted dress, they linger a long time on my breasts. I don't stop him but pick up my drink and sip from it again.

"I'm feeling rebellious tonight."

His eyes darken with a hunger at my words. "Anything I can assist you with?" He steps closer and I don't move until I spot King making his way towards us; he isn't happy.

King rudely pushes himself in between Marcus and me. Being subtle isn't a virtue my brother possesses.

"Excuse me." Marcus steps back and I place a hand on King's arms.

King looks at me and says unhappily, "Your husband is looking for you."

I want to roll my eyes. Instead, I pick up my drink and leave Marcus with King.

Damien is walking towards me and if I was a spectator here, I wouldn't take my eyes off him.

My heart trips as my eyes clash with his. His green eyes are on fire. I smile internally at his reaction. It's about time. His wide shoulders shift with each step he takes. He reaches me and leans in, my stomach twists as his cologne fills my senses. His cheek brushes mine. "What are you doing?" he growls in my ear. He smiles at me but the tightness around his eyes and in his jaw are visible to me.

"I have no idea what you mean?" I smile sweetly at him. His fingers wrap around my arm, the touch registers instantly with me. He steers me toward the back of the room. I peek up at Damien twice; he works a muscle in his jaw and for the first time fear skitters down my spine.

"Where are we going?" I quickly look behind me, but I don't see King or my father.

The lighting changes as we move into a dimmed corridor. My back collides with a wall and I'm stunned for a moment as Damien moves closer, boxing me in with his arms, planting them either side of my head.

"What do you want, Maria?" His growl surprises me.

I hold my head high against the slight amount of fear my brain registers. "I won't be ignored," I say for the hundredth time. My words fall flat as he moves closer. My heart pounds rapidly and I lower my lids before looking back up into Damien's eyes that are tightened around the edges. He looks angry.

"How could anyone ignore you?" His question confuses me. He ignores me all the time. My response is cut off as his lips slam down on mine. I have a moment of freezing under him before my body takes over and responds. My hands trail across his wide shoulders and I pull him closer. His tongue is warm as it snakes its way into my mouth. There is nothing gentle about the kiss and I take all he gives.

My ears ring as his hand moves down my side, everything buzzes but ceases as his fingers trail along the split in my dress that gives him access to my bare skin.

He turns his head away from my lips and continues kissing my neck, sending small sparks flying across my skin, leaving a burning path in its wake.

His long fingers push my underwear aside and I inhale deeply as he dips a finger inside me. I cling to his shoulders as he invades the sensitive area that's only ever been touched by me. A second finger slides in beside the first.

I groan into his neck, my body overwhelmed as he slides his wet fingers out, and drags them up to the bunch of nerves that jump, and have me biting on my lip to keep in another groan. I can't stop the sound as he slides his fingers into me, this time the force has me opening my eyes. The pain is instant and I become aware of the cold wall at my back, the sound of the party in the distance. Damien's fingers dance across my clit again and I'm dragged back under.

My breasts feel heavy and I pull him closer to me. His erection brushes against my abdomen and it brings me to the surface again, but I won't let go of this feeling that he is pulling out of me. His fingers plunge faster and harder, his movements hurt, and I'm lost between pain and pleasure. Pleasure wins out and moves to another height. My body sings and cries as Damien continues his assault on my pussy, and I fracture on his hand. Lights spark out and dwindle as he removes his hand and fixes my dress. He still stands close and I try to catch my breath.

"Will you behave now?"

My stunned mind tries to catch up with him. I gaze up at Damien as he takes a step back and I feel so exposed right now. My heart still beats wildly.

"Are you satisfied?" His growl has color scorching my cheeks. He's making it sound like he just did that to keep me happy instead of in a moment of passion.

"What?" Words fail me as he steps closer to me again.

"Don't ever seek attention from another man. If you want it that bad, I'll give it to you."

My throat tightens with humiliation at his words. The sting on my hand is instant as it connects with his face. My stomach tightens and his eyes widen briefly.

"You feel better now?" His growl has me wanting to hit him again.

"No. The only thing I feel is disgusted." I push away from him and he doesn't follow me as I try to piece myself back together before entering the party.

CHAPTER FOUR

DAMIEN

I can't let go of the rage that burns through me. My hands tighten around the yellow envelope that I pick up off the floor in the hallway. Maria kicks off her heels and gathers her dress in her hands as she races up the stairs. I have a moment of craving to follow her and finish what I started. My cock hardens and I quickly go into the kitchen before I take what I want. Opening the envelope, I know it's photos from the silky feel of the paper under my fingers. My eyes consume the image before I drop it on the table.

Leaving the kitchen, I stop at the hall table and get my gun. Tucking it into my waistband, I flick my jacket over it as I climb the stairs. The bathroom is flooded with light as I poke my head into the room. I don't enter, but make sure it's empty.

The image of Maria walking beside me through the mall has my chest tightening. Someone was following us that day and I missed it. I push open the next door carefully. The lights flood the gym. It's empty. Someone left these in our home.

"What are you doing?" Maria clutches her dress to her chest. I pull myself away from her wild brown eyes and check her room. I place a finger over my lips as I step fully into her room. Fear tightens her face, and I move around her and into her bathroom, it's empty. Opening her wardrobe, I'm circled by her perfume and the smell of soap. It's one that I identify as Maria. She clutches the dress to her chest like its armor.

"Stay here," I whisper as I leave her room and close the door behind me.

After I check the whole house, I return to the kitchen and go through the images. I allow myself to appreciate Maria, her long dark hair fanned out around her. The dark glasses cut me off from her stunning eyes. Everything about her from her long legs to her red lips is perfection.

"Damien!" Her shouts have me stuffing the photos back into the envelope. She continues to call me as I climb the stairs.

"I told you to stay quiet," I say the moment my eyes land on her. She hangs onto the door frame, the small piece of material that she calls nightwear barely covering her.

"No. You said stay here. What's going on?" She shrugs her small shoulders, her nose flaring with a temper she needs to reel in.

"I thought I heard something."

She releases the frame and steps out into the hall. My eyes drag across all her bare skin.

"You're lying." Her lips tug down at the corners.

I think of the images of her. She has no idea of the danger she's constantly in, but I understand why she wasn't informed before. Her whole life would have been her looking over her shoulder. Now that she's a woman, I feel she has a right to know.

"Go to sleep." I bark.

She's following me down the stairs, and I know if we reach the floor, this fight won't end. I stop abruptly and spin on the stairs, she stumbles and I grip her arm.

"Are you looking for attention again?"

My erection begs her to say yes.

She yanks her arm out of my hold. Through the small, thin fabric of her nightdress, her nipples harden and the temptation is almost too much for me to resist.

"Not from you." Her chest rises and falls and the anger that flashes in her eyes warns me she might strike me again. The sting of her fingers from earlier sparks to life and I want her more.

"Now who's lying?" I taunt. I have no idea why I am pushing her.

She turns and I tighten my fists so I don't drag her back to me. I don't move until she disappears. The slam of her door is my release and I move back down the stairs.

Gathering up the envelope, I pour myself a drink before sending a message to Nate, Jack, Charlie and Mattie to remind them our flight leaves in the morning for Rome.

I exhale loudly as I sit down with my drink. My face still stings from her earlier slap. I shift my shaft as it hardens. Anger laces its way through my arousal and I try to control the savage part of me, which wants to go upstairs and hurt her back. I finish the drink, trying to block out the images that dance dangerously close to becoming a reality.

We've boarded the plane. The morning had been stressful trying to avoid Maria as she poked at me in front of all the men. She is walking on thin ice with me. She's pushing me to the point of no return. On the plane she gives up. I placed her four seats away from me on our first class section of the plane. The space that normally held twenty people was only available to us. Nate lingers far too close to Maria—and once we return from Rome, it's something I intend to put a stop to. He's laughing and making her smile. His eyes meet mine and his smile slips from his face. I don't look away, the warning clear.

"You want a drink?" Charlie blocks my view of Nate for a moment and I look up at him.

He has a face that could melt snow. I don't think I've seen him smile. That's why he's part of my security team. One look at him and you would be running. His eyes promise pain.

"Yeah, just a beer," I say, and Nate fills my view again. He isn't laughing anymore. My gaze jumps to Maria and she's glaring at me. I can't stop the grin that tugs at my lips. She's ready to start again, so I cut her off by closing my eyes. I can sense her arrival before she starts.

"We need to talk."

I let my grin grow but keep my eyes closed. "Do we?"

"Your drink." I open my eyes and look at Maria as I take the beer from Charlie.

"Can I get you anything, Maria?" Charlie takes a swig from his own drink while he speaks to her

"No, Nate's getting me a beer." She smiles sweetly at Charlie and I see a ghost of a smile on his face. I sit up and Charlie moves into his seat as Nate arrives, taking a long swallow from the beer in his hand.

"I thought you were getting me one?" Maria stares at Nate's other empty hand. He holds out the beer he just drank from.

"Take mine."

Maria wraps her hand around the bottle and I'm standing. "After your mouth has been on it?" I say to Nate while taking the bottle from Maria. She's ready to go off again, but I slip my beer into her hand. She stares at it for a moment and when she raises it to her mouth and takes a deep drink, my trousers tighten.

"Go get me a fresh one." I hand Nate back his bottle and his face tightens.

"Ladies and gentlemen, the Captain has turned on the Fasten Seat Belt sign. If you haven't already done so, please stow your carry-on luggage underneath the seat in front of you, or in an overhead bin. Please take your seat and fasten your seat belt. And also, make sure your seat and folding trays are in their full, upright position."

Nate grins. "Sorry, I have to take my seat." He's being a little shit.

"We remind you that this is a non-smoking flight. Smoking is prohibited on the entire aircraft, including the lavatories. Tampering with, disabling or destroying the lavatory smoke detectors is prohibited by law."

I strap myself in and look up to find Maria watching me. Her belt is on. Nate sits in beside her.

Jack and Mattie are already in their seats.

"Thank you for flying with Lake Airlines." The flight attendant ends her announcement. Flying isn't something I enjoy. I keep my eyes closed and try not to grip the armrest. I hope my pose makes anyone who looks at me believe I'm relaxed.

The airplane tears down the runway and I'm preparing myself for the moment we are airborne, my ears ring and my stomach shifts. Once we are leveled out, all my senses relax. I don't open my eyes immediately.

The flight attendant announces we can remove our belts and I do so. I open my eyes but don't look to Maria, instead, I move in beside Charlie so I'm facing away from them.

"These were left at my house." I hand him the yellow envelope of photos.

I observe Charlie's reaction as he slips them out. His eyes dart across the image before flicking up to me.

"I found them in my kitchen. Whoever took them was in my house." Charlie nods and returns his attention to the image.

"We need to be extra careful and even when we return, I'll want you around."

Laughter from Maria has me wanting to wrap my hands around Nate's neck.

"Have you any ideas?" Charlie draws me back to him. He places the photos back in the envelope.

"Her family has more enemies than friends." It could be anyone. I take the envelope back from Charlie.

"You could be the target."

I nod my head. "I had thought of that." I have a lot of enemies too. Working for two very powerful men does that.

"But she's the center point of each photo." Her father told me she had attracted the attention of a rival organization in the south of the country. They wanted Maria to marry their son and strengthen the bonds, but Kane refused. Marrying me took her out of the limelight—and kept her safe, too.

But I know they might resurface, and that's who I'm putting my money on. I can't tell my men the truth; that information is between Maria's father, King, and me.

"I'll keep a closer watch." Charlie reassures me.

Jack sits in the seat I had recently been in. "I always wanted to see the Vatican." He looks from me to Charlie. Jack's a bodybuilder like Charlie, they both work out at the same gym but I don't think they have any other association with each other, apart from working for me and Kane.

They are chalk and cheese. Jack takes pride in his appearance and always wears a smile. I like that about him. He's the underdog. Anyone who looks at him sees all muscle and no brain. They're wrong. He's lethal.

"This isn't a sightseeing exhibition."

He raises a dark brow. "If Maria wants to go, then I get to see it?"

"She doesn't," I say instantly.

"She is the cat's mother. If you want to ask me something, Jack, you know you can."

I don't turn at the sweet sound of Maria's voice.

Jack's smile splits his face. "I was telling your husband that I want to see the Vatican." The word husband sounds so strange. I don't think I'll ever get used to it.

"What did my husband say?" Her hand rests close to my head as she speaks to Jack.

"He said you don't want to see it. So, now I can't."

"Is that so?" I can hear the joy in Maria's words. She leans down and I glance at her. Her face is close to mine, so close I can see the different shades of brown in her stunning eyes. I'm aware of my hands resting on the armrest, the want to touch her has me holding still.

"Liar," she declares, standing up. That one word is wrapped in layers.

"The Vatican will be our first stop, Jack."

He's smiling as she walks away, but it dissolves when his eyes meet mine. Maria is my Achilles heel, and all my men know it.

"Go sit somewhere else," I say, and he grins as he leaves me.

I hear Nate and Maria's laughter. It grates on me, but something is telling me that's exactly what she is trying to do.

CHAPTER FIVE

MARIA

I'm laughing louder than necessary. Nate isn't funny at all. I feel stretched and the plane is suffocating me right now. I'm ready to get out of my seat. I'm so distracted that I don't see Damien coming towards us. His looming form sends trepidation racing across my already tightened skin.

"Get up." I'm ready to look behind me to see who he is talking to, but he leans in. When his fingers circle my arm, his touch is gentle, a complete contradiction to what I'm seeing.

"What?" My confusion entwines with my words as he brings me to the front of the plane.

Charlie nods at me before his attention is consumed by his phone.

"Sit down, Maria."

I glare at Damien and he doesn't blink. I slide into the seat and he sandwiches himself beside me. "Why am I sitting here?" I challenge him.

He's stiff—like if I poke him he might crack.

His warning glare has me wanting to know even more.

"Damien?" I turn in my chair so I'm facing him.

"Your laugh is distracting everyone from their work."

Once again he manages to stump me. He can't be serious?

"When I married you, I didn't do it to go from one controlling situation to another."

Damien looks amused.

My blood boils. "I can't even breathe with you." My outburst has everyone looking at me and I hate it. I hate all of it. I'm up and it's like everyone leans toward me waiting to see which minion Damien sends after me. I spin around ready to tell them it will not be any of them, and nearly smack into Damien.

"It's a plane. I can't go anywhere. Or do anything." I'm all fired up and I have no way to blow off the anger that bubbles through me. "I can't even laugh. Is everyone working now?" I don't let Damien answer. "No. They are all too busy watching you make an ass of yourself." My mouth is running away with itself, but he asked for it.

"Maria." He growls a warning.

I throw caution to the wind. "No..." My words are cut off as Damien places his large hand across my mouth.

"Shhh."

I'm gobsmacked as he takes his hand off my mouth and moves around me. When I look up I see everyone looking at me.

Nate grins.

"Have you no work to do?" I bark and he slides back down in his chair with a stupid grin on his face. In a plane there aren't many places to storm to. Charlie gets up and I move to the side to let him pass. He acts like he didn't see anything. My cheeks are still warm and I need to sit down.

A yellow envelope catches my attention that's tucked along the side of Damien's chair. I glance at the curtain that he just left through, before moving like I'm not in a rush. Mattie has headphones on and Jack has his eyes closed, but I can tell he isn't asleep. I consider pretending to look for something but my worked up body cuts through the pretense, and I openly wrap my fingers around Damien's envelope. My heart stutters when I turn around and my eyes clash with Jack's grinning face.

I dare him to say anything. He doesn't and I turn on my heel and slide into an empty seat. Pictures slip out onto my lap. There's a moment when my heart rate shoots up, it's not the photo...it's Damien. It's how he's looking at me. His vibrant green eyes are focused on me like there is nothing else around us. My gaze darts over to me. The skirt looks shorter than I remembered, but it works. We look good together. My attention shoots back to Damien, he looks like someone you wouldn't mess with. His black suit fits him perfectly; it hangs from wide shoulders and covers his perfect tall frame. He made me appear tiny beside him.

My hand tightens on the photo, I know he's arrived back. I can sense Damien behind me and his cologne gave him away. I slide the photos back into the envelope and now I'm wondering who took them and why? Once I have them all back in, I turn in my seat to face him and hand him the envelope. I don't feel bad for snooping.

Green eyes bore into me and I try not to squirm under the heaviness of Damien's stare. He takes the envelope much too calmly from my hands and walks away. I frown. It's all too calm.

"Why is someone taking photos of me?" I'm pushing out the seat. Everyone's attention once again is fixated on me.

Damien ignores me as he pulls down his overhead baggage.

"Is someone following me?" I stare at his wide back.

Radio silence.

"You better answer me quickly."

Damien removes something that jingles from his bag and when he turns to me, I'm expecting an answer. He takes a step towards me and I take one back. Something sparkles in his hands before I land in a seat.

"What are you..." My words are cut off as he takes my arm and slaps a handcuff on it, before attaching it to the sidebar on the seat. I yank my arm.

"Unlock me now."

He squats down so we are eye level and my stomach rises and dives.

"You don't touch someone else's property."

His words have me yanking my arm again. "I'm going to get really loud if you don't ...." He stands, cutting off my words as he removes the tie from his neck.

"What are you doing?" I try to move away from him as far as my arm will allow.

He easily grips my shoulder. "Will I gag you?" He growls.

My mouth hangs open and I close it quickly while shaking my head. My heart is dancing too fast. Too many thoughts twirl with my anger.

"Good." He grins at me as he stands. He doesn't replace his tie and I grit my teeth as he walks away. Nate fills my vision from across the way. He isn't looking amused and I'm glad someone is on my side. I yank my arm again and the noise sounds too loud.

Nate gets out of his seat and from the set of his shoulders I know that he's going to say something. I should stop him, I really should, but I don't.

"I'll keep an eye on her; there is no need to handcuff her." I cringe at his words. Does he really think he would just hand over the key?

I pull my arm as far as I can and try to see over the seats, I can see the crown of Damien's head.

"No." Damien was back to his good old one-word answers. I sit back in the seat.

"Kane won't be happy." My stomach squeezes as Nate mentions my father's name. Would he care? They have this illusion of my family like they would go through fire for me, and that's how it looks on the outside. But they'd do anything to keep me under lock and key. I don't think my father would be all that outraged over Damien handcuffing me. Right now, I can imagine him smiling, saying he did the right thing. Anything to keep me safe and out of trouble.

"Nate," I call him before he gets in trouble. I sit half up and this time Damien looks at me and I sink back down in my seat. I kick out at the air with irritation.

"When we get back, why don't you tell him?" Damien's response has someone sneering. I'm picturing Jack, he doesn't seem to like Nate.

"I just think..." Nate starts.

Damien cuts him off. "I don't pay you to think. You're doing too much of it lately." The warning in Damien's voice reaches my ears.

I hear the footsteps before I lean out of my seat. Nate sits down and I want to thank him for trying, but he won't look at me. My skin buzzes with rebellion. I can't sit still, so I lie back across the three seats, my arm pulls painfully.

"I need to go to the bathroom," I shout while closing my eyes. I want my freedom back. A latte would be nice, or another cold beer.

No response. "I need to go to the bathroom now," I shout louder. Closing my eyes, I'm ready to bring the plane down. When I open them, my heart pounds as Damien shadows me, but I know he won't let me sit here if I need to go to the bathroom. I try to hide my satisfaction of getting the upper hand. It's short lived as he leans in with a secret grin on his lips. My stomach hollows at his closeness, and I ignore the heavy steel around my wrist. and think about the charity party and what it felt like to have his lips on me. His fingers inside me, I squeeze my legs together.

His long fingers touch my face and my heart palpitates as I get lost in my want for him. He leans his head in closer and I think he's going to kiss me. I see a flash of white before material fills my mouth and I'm trying to spit it out. Damien works faster than what should be humanly possible, and tightens his tie around the gag in my mouth. Shock rushes to the surface and I'm shouting, my words muffled by the material. I'm reaching up to pull it off. Damien moves away from me, un-cuffing me from the side bar. I'm confused until he drags me closer, and wraps the chain of the cuffs through the bar, before clamping the cuff on my other wrist. When he's done, he grins at me while tightening the tie around my face, that I managed to get slightly off. It burns as hair gets caught in the knot he's made.

"You were warned."

Heat scorches my face and I rattle the chain while screaming. He isn't fazed as he walks away. I kick the chair and scream, but no one moves. Hair sticks to the side of my face that's overheated and it itches. I let out a half cry as I push my head into my shoulder to try to move some of the hair. Another scream tears from me, my face grows itchier. His cologne tingles my nose that rises from the tie. I can't move as I'm too close to the seat and I just want to curl up.

I give another scream, trying to get Nate's attention. I grow silent when he looks at me. What can he do? Nothing. I shake my head, trying to tell him it doesn't matter. His brow draws down and his fingers curl into fists.

I shake my head again, trying to tell him to forget. His body grows tighter and I look away from him. My heart still races and I'm clammy. Closing my eyes, I shut off the world and try to calm my heart. My rage keeps making it race but as time passes and no one comes near me, I go from anger to tiredness.

It's like a beacon of light as the flight attendant steps into the walkway. I'm screaming and yanking at my wrists and I know I've won when I see the horror in her eyes.

CHAPTER SIX

DAMIEN

I'm putting the photos back in the envelope, when I hear Maria kicking up a storm again. She had to get points for not giving up, but I'm wondering what set her off. The flight attendant stands beside her, her face growing paler by the second.

Shit.

"She's perfectly fine." I smile as I stand and walk towards her. "She isn't mentally stable." I inform the air hostess.

Maria grows still and I can almost feel the heat rise off her.

"Oh." The air hostess looks unsure, but I've captured her attention. I widen my smile and color enters her cheeks.

"I'm responsible for her safety. She doesn't like flying and often acts out." I glance down at Maria. If she could breathe fire, we'd all be cinders.

The air hostess follows my gaze and she steps away from Maria, who looks feral right now.

"This is for her safety and the passengers on the plane."

The flight attendant exhales loudly while bobbing her head like she gets it.

"It's a good thing you are here." A hand rests on my arm and Maria's attention is consumed with the movement.

"Thank you." I glance down at her name tag. "Lorraine."

She blushes and giggles at me using her name.

Maria starts mumbling again.

The overhead belt sign comes on and Lorraine's eyes grow wide. "Oh, yes. Everyone, we will be getting ready for landing." She's flustered and when her eyes land on me she smiles again.

"Thank you, Lorraine."

"You're welcome..."

"Damien." I fill in the gap.

She laughs softly.

Maria starts rattling her handcuffs and her muffles grow louder.

"I'd better see to her," I say to Lorraine, who walks away and starts checking on the rest of the first class passengers while flipping up tables and double checking the overhead doors. I stand and smile at her until she leaves this section of the plane.

My smile falls and I glare at Maria. Her wrists are red from her yanking so much and I grit my teeth. Reaching into my pocket, I take the key out and her eyes are fixated on it as I push it into the cuff. The click has her eyes widening, but I don't remove it. She's ready to run, I can see it in her eyes. I remove it quickly and snap it onto my own wrists. She yanks the steel causing it to burn.

With her free hand she pulls off the gag. Her cheeks are rosy, her hair plastered to her face and her innocence calls to me. My cock twitches and it all shatters as she opens her pretty mouth.

"You will pay for that." She's pulling strands of hair angrily from her face, my tie hangs around her neck and it teases me. My body tightens and I start to walk away. She has no choice but to follow, but she doesn't make it easy. Every few seconds my wrists burn but I keep moving. When I reach my seat I sit down and she still hasn't learned her lesson as she stands.

"Sit down, Maria." I warn as I shift in the seat.

"You are all fired." She's telling Jack and Mattie, who glance at her for a second before they return to buckling themselves in. I pull on her arm and she stumbles into her seat. I balance her so she doesn't fall and she tries to tug away from me only to remember we are cuffed together. It's hard getting my belt on as Maria jerks her arm every second, but I manage to get it clipped in. Maria buckles herself in, wrenching my wrist, and I close my eyes. I keep my hands relaxed, the fact that they want to grip the handrests have me aware of my movements.

"You all lost your jobs." She sings again beside me. No one is paying attention to her. They work for me, not her. She has no power over them and they know it, soon she will too.

The descent starts and I hold still. "My father will sack every one of you." She's still ranting beside me and I want to tell her to shut up. The plane wobbles and I hold still, trying hard to not wrap my hand around the hand rest.

It's over quick and when we land, Maria remains quiet even as I undo the cuffs. I am under no illusion that she has decided to behave. I can see the wheels turning in her head as she plots and plans my demise. Right now

I don't care. Getting off the plane has me breathing for the first time in five hours.

Once we get our luggage, we leave the airport. Our transport is waiting. Maria doesn't speak a word and glares out the window for the entire ride. Her anger bubbles under the surface. Nate's watching her and he is becoming a huge problem. His eyes meet mine and I'm amused at the level of anger I see. I allow a grin to tug at my lips and he wisely looks away.

We arrive at our hotel, the door is opened for us, and I am glad to get out of the car. Maria jumps out and I circle my hand around her wrist. Her head snaps up to me and I hope she can read the warning in my eyes.

"Nate, get the bags," I say without taking my eyes off Maria. Once I release her, she rubs her wrist like I'd hurt her. I had intentionally made my touch gentle. She's just looking for attention again.

The white marble lobby floor makes our footsteps echo around the large space. I'm grateful for the cool air. We are greeted by a wide-smiling receptionist. His welcome is quick and hard to understand with his accent. King bed. I hear those two words and apparently so does Maria.

"No thank you," she says.

The receptionist's eyes dart away from the slip of paper I'm about to sign for the rooms and at Maria.

"Sorry Madam, that is all we have."

"I am not sharing a bed with him." She points at me.

"Maria," I warn.

"No. No way. It's not happening. Ever."

The receptionist looks lost as his eyes ping from me to Maria. "I am so sorry Madam, but all our rooms are booked up."

"I want a different room now. I don't care how you do it, but do it."

She's drawing attention to us and I'm tired from all her outbursts. I sign the papers and take the keys off the desk.

"I'm not staying with you." She's shouting now.

"She's drunk. She had way too much on the plane." I tell the receptionist as I take her arm.

"Get off me!" she's barking, as I direct her to the elevator and hit the button.

"I'm speaking to you, Damien. You can't just manhandle me whenever you want." The ding of the doors has me shoving her in. I reach for the button that will close the doors. Her eyes grow wide as I advance on her and the world is cut off behind us.

I corner her, placing a hand to her left. My right hand grips her chin before sliding to her neck, I'm aware not to put pressure on it, I tell myself not to squeeze, not to hurt her.

"When will you learn?"

Her breath comes out harshly and fans across my face.

The door opens and I know it's my men. I glance at them over my shoulder but I don't release Maria. "Take the next one." I bark and wait a few seconds until the door closes again. I catch Nate's eye and something deep burns in them. He has feelings for her, he doesn't like how she's been treated.

I didn't expect to have a vixen on my hands. I didn't think she would fight against this marriage. Maria keeps her hands at her side, but fear blossoms in her brown eyes. "I will lock you in your room for the rest of this trip if you don't behave." My thumb strokes her neck and she jumps a little. I see lust mingling with fear in her eyes.

My hand tightens on her throat and I push myself closer to her. I want to cut off the air from her lungs and watch the pain burn her. My belt feels heavy around my trousers. It's one of my favorite tools to use during sex. I release my hold on her and exhale loudly, trying to control the raging blood that's pounding in my cock.

"I don't want to lock you up, Maria. You understand?" Tying her up is all I want to do.

My eyes trail to her lips that she licks. The thought of her tongue around my cock has my hand tightening once again. Her breasts brush my chest and I lean in allowing her to feel my erection. Her eyes widen. "Is that what this is all about? You want me to touch you?"

Her breathing grows heavier, her want has her pushing her body towards mine. I grin. "If you're a good girl, I might make you cum."

She's fighting and struggling. "I don't want you near me."

My grin turns into a laugh. "Oh, Maria, you are such a liar."

Her face grows red and she shoves me, igniting the darkness in me. I want to inflict pain on her, bring her to a height where pain and pleasure entwine themselves together, and you can't think what it is you're getting high on. I release her abruptly and move away before I hurt her. She's breathing heavily. Looking up at her, she rubs her neck.

"You have no right to put your hands on me." She's barking again.

I turn away from her and hit the floor number. I need to get out of this space. My body hums with a want and I tighten my jaw.

"Your father can't pay me half enough to stay." I grind out the words. This isn't in the agreement. Her silence has me looking at her. Brown eyes waver like I've hurt her somehow.

That pain turns into malice. "I can't say the same thing. The ten million was the only reason I agreed to this. Otherwise, I wouldn't have given you a second glance."

Her words sting me. It was arranged. It was about money, I know that. It shouldn't fucking hurt.

The elevator doors open and she storms from them. I tighten my jaw as I follow her. Charlie is up ahead. I easily catch up to Maria and touch her lower back, her spine straightens and she tries to outrun my touch.

"Can you stay with her?" I hand Charlie the keys to the room and he nods. He's the only one I trust. I don't pause but move further down the hall. I have no idea where I am going, all I know is I need to get away from Maria and the want that burns through me to hurt her.

CHAPTER SEVEN

MARIA

"**G**et out of my room," I say to Charlie as I open my suitcase on my bed. I want privacy, I want a moment to compose myself.

"I'm afraid that's not possible."

I glare at him as I slam my suitcase lid closed. It's unsatisfactory. I stomp past Charlie and slam the bathroom door. The bang rattles the frame and I feel a bit better. I'm not one to have a temper, but Damien brings out the worst in me. My breasts are still heavy with want and I push it down, hating myself for wanting him so badly. The worst part is that he knows that he could have me in a second. I need to show more restraint. I half laugh at that. If he wants me, I don't think I can stop him. My body responds to him too easily. He's gorgeous. A gorgeous asshole.

I run the shower and return to the bedroom to get my night clothes. After traveling and being handcuffed, I'm ready to end this day.

"Can I have some privacy?" I say to Charlie, not expecting him to give it to me.

"I'll be outside the door." His monotone doesn't make me believe that he doesn't care or that he might become complacent. If Charlie is watching over me, I know I won't get an inch away before being brought back here.

I strip out of my clothes and enjoy the water's spray. Red marks blossom on my wrists and I rub them gently with shower gel. He has marked me. My stomach twists at the thought. I close my eyes against the horror that is rising in me. My hand automatically touches my neck that he squeezed. My own fingers tighten around it and I stop what I am doing. My heart pounds and I don't understand what's wrong with me.

I liked it. I liked his large hands hurting me, marking me. Touching me.

I quickly wash away my confusion. I've never had sex or any kind of foreplay. Maybe that's part of it, or maybe I'm just getting confused between what's normal and what isn't.

I pull on my nightdress and poke my head out into my room expecting to see Charlie there. He isn't. I return and grab my toothbrush and brush my teeth as I walk around the bedroom. It's beautifully furnished and the beige and cream color scheme makes me think of Rome. Two large white pillars dominate the middle of our bedroom. A small white table stands beside one and I pluck an apple from it. Returning to the bathroom, I rinse my mouth out and leave my toothbrush there before taking the apple out onto the balcony. I have a clear view, we are so close to the Vatican. The hotel is right inside Vatican city, its white sprawling walls encircles us. I had randomly picked Rome when Nate had asked me where I wanted to go. I never actually thought the next day I would be standing on a balcony overlooking the city.

The lights blink in and out and it curbs my anger. Each moment I spend outside in the warm night breeze calms me. The door opens and smashes into my calm.

"I'm not going to climb down the seven floors, Charlie." I lean over the balcony. We're seven floors high, I counted them properly.

My stomach twists. Damien's cologne circles me as he steps out onto the balcony. His gaze skitters across all my bare skin and I have a lot showing. The apple weighs heavily in my hand and I have a moment of wanting to throw it at him. I bring it to my mouth and take a bite. His eyes are fixated on my movements and he blinks, smashing the moment before looking out over the city. My stomach tumbles as he takes a step closer, shoving his hands in his pockets.

I chew the unwanted apple and take another bite, the noise seems so loud in the silence of the night.

"Have you calmed down?"

I glare at his side profile. "About what exactly?" I take another bite and make sure it's louder. His head snaps to me, his eyes trailing to my lips. The strap of my nightdress slips off my shoulder and I don't move to fix it. His eyes burn my skin and I hold in a shiver that wants to shake my body.

"The fact that you handcuffed me?" His eyes keep flicking to my braless breasts. They feel heavy with his gaze upon them. My body grows more aware of him the longer he stands there.

"Maybe the fact that you gagged me?"

His grin is instant. My heart picks up as he steps closer. His eyes tell a million stories that his lips refuse to say.

"Maybe the fact that you put your hands on me." I swallow around the lie. I didn't mind him doing that. His eyes skim across my throat and I find myself leaning back so I can keep eye contact, and allow him to see the mark on my neck. He reaches for me, his large hand touches my neck gently. This time I can't stop the shiver that assaults my body.

"I think you liked me doing all that to you, Maria." His words have me aware of the weight of my body.

His thumb strokes back and forth and my core clenches. His lips become my sole focus and I'm tempted to stand up on the tip of my toes and press a kiss against them. Damien moves us backwards.

"I think you like when I control you." His hand tightens slightly on my throat, and fear jumps up my throat. I clench my fists so I don't stop him. I'm dancing with the devil and I'm not sure of the outcome. My shoulders hunch forward as my back touches the cool glass of the balcony doors. He's towering over me, making me smaller by the second.

His hand loosens on my throat and I don't want this to stop. I want his hands on me. I step into him and press my lips against his. He responds to me immediately and I'm the one in control, as I cling to his broad shoulders, pulling him closer until I feel his huge erection against my abdomen. I groan with anticipation. His lips slide from mine and he spins me. His cock nestles against my ass. My eyes clash with his in the glass. My heart pounds as his hand tightens around my throat, I tilt my head back giving him as much access as he needs. I can't look away from his hungry eyes as he slips his hand under my nightdress and pulls my under pants aside.

"Look at yourself, Maria." The whispered words have me growing wetter and I groan out loud as he slips his fingers inside me. I feel sinful as he strokes my clit while plunging his fingers inside me. His hand grows tighter around my throat as his fingers move faster. The air grows thinner and I struggle between panic and pleasure. "Come for me." His words break through the swirling veil that's coating me and I'm so close. His body grinds tighter against mine, his cock prodding my ass as his fingers dance along my clit.

"Look at me."

I open my eyes and refocus on Damien. I'm toeing the line between dream and reality. I can't breathe as my body demands release and tightens before snapping. I cry out and his hand loosens as I cum all over his fingers. The shocks continue as I gasp for air. I can't take my eyes off the man who still holds me. The hunger on Damien's face is slightly frightening. His fingers leave my pussy and he slides my underwear back in place.

"Good girl, Maria."

I don't feel like a good girl. I feel like a very sinful woman. His hand trails from my neck and brushes my swollen breasts. His erection is still pressed against my ass and now it scares me. It's too big.

He releases me fully and steps back, and the shy part of me wants to keep facing the glass. But the inexperienced and awed part of me turns and faces him. He eliminates the small space between us and I have an overwhelming urge to step into his arms and wrap myself up in him.

His fingers trail up my arm and I shiver while closing my eyes. He lifts the strap and slides it back up onto my shoulder.

"Get some sleep."

My eyes spring open as a soft warm breeze fills the space that he steps away from. He steps into the bedroom and I'm left a bit frazzled and a part of me is unsatisfied. I follow him.

"I want to touch you."

He pulls off his tie, and I think of him using it earlier on me. He opens the top three buttons of his shirt painfully slow, but stops there.

"Go to sleep." He repeats his earlier words.

"Why can't I touch you?" I step closer to him.

He closes me off by turning his back on me. "I don't want you to."

His words wrap around me and my heart races. He doesn't want me. Tears that I refuse to shed burn my eyes.

"You're such a liar." I call him out and he glares at me, a warning flashes in his eyes. I smile. "What are you afraid of?" I'm poking the bear, I know it, but I refuse to accept that I can't touch him.

"I'm tired, Maria." He steps away from me and into the bathroom.

I'm unsure what to do. The rebellious part of me wants to follow him. I march to the bed and take two pillows, firing them onto the floor.

"Well, sleep tight darling." I sneer as I pull off the throw and fling it onto the floor. "You're sleeping on the floor," I bark. My temper is rising the longer he ignores me. "Are you ignoring me so I'll come into the bathroom?" I ask as I climb up on the bed.

I freeze as he walks out of the bathroom. He's wearing a white t-shirt and a pair of green boxers, and I can't look away. I'm growing wet again and the pillows and blankets on the floor feel unnecessary.

"I was sleeping on the floor, anyway." His erection has made a huge tent in his boxers, he doesn't try to hide it as he gathers up the pillows and blanket.

I throw myself back on the bed and lie still as he gets settled. Once the room grows silent, my mind gets loud. I want to ask him why he doesn't want me to touch him. I turn on my side and stare at the white-washed wall. Men always look at me with a desire in their eyes, it's how I learned to use my body to bend the rules, but it always only goes so far. Men appreciate me with their eyes and that's it. A relationship with a male never goes any further. But Damien doesn't have to fear King or my father. I'm his wife. He can take what he wants from me.

I turn to the other side of the huge bed. A vase of white flowers catches my eye. They look fluffy. I've never seen flowers like them before. I sit up and glare down at Damien, he has his back to me but I can see his large profile.

"I want a dog."

He doesn't move a muscle.

"Damien, I want a dog."

"Go to sleep." His words are growled and I like getting a reaction.

"No."

He glowers at me over his shoulder but it melts into a grin that has me clutching the quilt. I'm excited, but fear skitters down my back.

He turns away from me and I sense I've pushed as far as I can tonight. Lying back, I close my eyes and try to fall asleep.

Waking up to an empty room isn't fun, but I shower again and get dressed for the day. A long, black, maxi dress covers most of my body. Grabbing a large straw hat and a black shawl, along with my day bag, I leave the hotel room.

"Good morning."

I stall as Nate smiles at me. "Were you lingering outside my room?" I ask, pulling the door behind me.

"No, I was walking past getting ready to go have breakfast."

I step up beside him. "Is that so?" I ask with a smile.

His smile widens. "What are we doing today?"

We start to walk to the row of elevators. "Jack wants to see the Vatican, so that's our first stop."

The doors open and I let an elderly couple out before entering. Nate leans across me and hits the ground floor.

"I could have done that," I say at his closeness.

"I got it." His smile is quick. "I want to see the Trevi Fountain."

The elevator descends and I try not to grin at Nate. "You're a big boy, go see it then."

The elevator stops and I move forward for the doors to open.

"That I am."

I look at Nate from the corner of my eye and see the smirk I'm expecting to see.

The dining space is buzzing with people. I see Mattie, Charlie and Jack a few tables away. Jack waves at me and I tip my head towards him. His huge frame is intimidating and he's captured the attention of a five-year-old girl who is eating a slice of toast while gawking at him. He must look like the hulk to her.

"What do you want?" Nate asks while he picks up a plate and starts to load everything and anything onto it.

My eyes dance around the room again and I feel disappointed when I don't see Damien.

I pick up a croissant. "I'll have this."

I put it on a plate to take it with me and get myself a glass of orange juice.

"That's not going to fill you," Nate says while he follows me to the table with his buffet.

"If I'm still hungry, I'm sure you can give me some of yours." I slide in beside Jack. "You have an admirer," I tell him as I put my glass and plate on the table.

His smile lights up his blue eyes. "It's hard to miss her."

I glance at the little girl and smile. Her head snaps towards her parents like she can't believe she was caught.

"How did you sleep?" Nate starts arranging his buffet across from me. The other men don't speak to him and I wonder for the first time how they all get on. I've never had them all with me at once. But I grew up around them. If we were at home, they would never sit with me. King wouldn't allow this kind of interaction.

"Okay." I focus on my croissant as I answer. The pastry grows heavy in my mouth as I look up to see Damien enter the dining room. His suit fits his large frame perfectly and if I didn't know him, I would think he owned the hotel. No, I would think he owned the world. His eyes skip over the crowd and when they land on me, I swallow around the pastry. Nate shifts, looking over his shoulder, and Damien's eyes jump to him before he dismisses him, and walks to the buffet area.

I swallow down the dough with a mouthful of orange juice. I can't take my eyes off him as he walks to our table with the smallest mug of coffee. The aroma hits me instantly as he sits down.

Everyone except Nate greets Damien. He pulls up a chair, so he's at the end of the table. I clock the wedding band on his finger and my own feels heavy now. I touch the back of the bands with my thumb. My body is responding to him and I shift in my seat.

"So what's on the agenda today, boss?" Jack asks while stuffing a rasher into his mouth.

"First the Vatican for you," I answer and I'm waiting for Damien to interject but he doesn't. He sips his coffee while watching me.

"Thank you, Maria." Jack's smile is sweet.

How can I resist? "Is your fan still watching?" I ask him.

He peeks over a huge arm. "Yeah." His smile is nice and warm and I'm surprised to see Damien smile. It slips from his face when his eyes clash with mine.

"Then the Trevi Fountain for Nate." Damien takes another sip of his coffee and I glance at Nate who won't lift his head from his plate. I frown at him, but he just keeps shoving food into his mouth.

"You want to see the Trevi Fountain?" Damien asks him and he finally looks up. His eyes waver with uncertainty.

"I don't mind."

I want to call him out, but something in the way he holds himself, has me finishing my orange juice, as we all get ready to leave. Finally, Nate looks at me, and I'm surprised with the amount of anger his eyes hold. I just don't know if that anger is towards me or Damien.

CHAPTER EIGHT

DAMIEN

Maria stares around her and she's so taken with architecture. While she gawks at it, I use the time to watch her. Her confidence is always on the surface, but the depths that her innocence runs is what initially drew me to her. She is the deepest lake—one that I want to swim—and that scares me.

She scares me.

"Father." She smiles as a priest walks past us. His eyes meet mine and he quickly looks away.

Once he's out of sight I'm waiting for Maria to ask. She has no filter. I don't think anyone ever advised her she should have one.

"I thought you were a Catholic?" We walk around large stone columns.

"I am," I answer.

She sucks in a lip and my mind stays where it has since I saw her at breakfast. All I want is to bury myself inside her. I need to relieve myself when we get back to the hotel. It might relieve some of the want and pain that is growing hourly in my trousers.

"You didn't greet the priest." She pulls the black shawl tighter around her slim shoulders.

"He's not my father. He's a man with a collar."

She frowns at my answer.

"I went to an all boy school run by priests," I explain.

Her frown deepens.

I glance around me to see Jack taking photos with his phone. I have never seen him so excited. Mattie walks around, his eyes always touching each of us. When he looks at me, I call him over with a nod of my head.

"Okay, so what? They were strict?"

I look to Maria and her question is heavy, but it's the eagerness in her eyes that makes me answer.

"No, they were violent bastards."

She grows still, her hand clutches her throat. My trousers grow tighter.

"Can you stay with Maria? I need to have a word with Charlie."

Mattie is the oldest and the only other one of us who's married. His eyes are always hooded with anger, but I've never seen him act on that anger.

Charlie looks as uninterested as I feel. The envelope in my suit jacket feels heavy now, and I try to control my need at the imprint of the images.

"I woke up to someone sliding an envelope under the door." I glance at Charlie and we both stand shoulder to shoulder facing the alcove that allows people to stop and pray. "By the time I got out the door, they were gone."

I glance at Charlie, feeling a sense of frustration. I went straight to the security room and had them play back the footage. A dark figure with a black cap drawn down had delivered them. Not once did he look up. He was aware of each camera.

"Someone followed us."

I nod at Charlie. "Why?" I can't understand it.

The images were of me and Maria on the balcony. The photographer had captured her pleasure beautifully. There were ten different shots—from us talking, to kissing; me making her cum...and all the way to the moment she was standing by herself on the balcony. She's wearing a look and I'm not sure if it's sadness or fear.

"One of the photo's had words scrawled on the back." I glance at Charlie again. "Telling me not to touch her."

It makes no sense. Why would someone follow us, take pictures and warn me away from my wife?

I know touching her isn't allowed, but this isn't Kane or King. If they knew, I don't think they would be taking photos, they would take a body part.

I glance at Maria, I'm playing with fire touching her and someone knows that. My gaze moves around the room to my number one suspect. Nate.

"You think it's Nate?" Charlie follows my line of sight.

"I'm not sure."

"He's taken with her." Charlie admits.

"Keep this between us and just be extra vigilant." Everyone with a camera right now was a suspect. But Nate had made the top of my list.

I ask Rodger, our tech guy to get me all he has on Nate.

Maria talks to Mattie and he scratches his head while smiling at her. She's infectious. Her animated face has me turning away and taking out my phone. I have nothing from Rodger. I want it to be Nate so I can end this. All it would take is those photos being sent to King or Kane to place my head on the chopping board. I exhale and walk back to Maria. Her words slow as she takes me in.

I nod to Mattie and he leaves us.

"What were you talking to Charlie about?" Her curiosity has her glancing around for Charlie before her eyes settle on me.

"Football."

She frowns at me. "Why are you always so hostile?"

I remove the space between us and I love how Maria never shies away from me. "Why are you always so nosy?"

Her nose curls up. "If you weren't so secretive, I wouldn't have to ask a million questions."

My lips tug up. "I'm not secretive, I just have a filter. It's something you don't have."

She smiles and shrugs. "I don't think that's a bad thing."

Normally it is, but on her it's perfect.

"I never lie," she says and I hear the undercurrent to her words. Implying that I do.

"I don't lie either. I withhold the truth. There is a difference." I want to kiss her but I'm aware of everyone around us. I'm aware of each camera that could capture this moment.

Her laughter surprises me. "No. You bend and twist it to your will."

Her playful tone is making me step away from her. It would be easy to enjoy her company. "Finish up your sightseeing."

I shut her down and she narrows her eyes at me. She's ready to fight. I can see it in her brown eyes.

"We are in a church," I remind her. She takes her religion seriously.

"Like you care." She marches off and I keep close to her but she doesn't speak, and I don't think she takes anything else in. Guilt churns in my stomach, but as I glance around the space and meet Nate's eyes, I think keeping my distance from her is important.

We don't stay much longer at the Vatican. "Are we going to the Trevi Fountain now?" Maria's excitement has resurfaced since we left the Vatican and got into a cab. Her happiness has me rethinking my decision as the car zooms back towards the hotel.

"No." Nate stiffens across from us. He's sandwiched in between Charlie and Jack. He looks uncomfortable, and so he should.

The car pulls up at the hotel and Maria is scrambling for the door. She pulls off the hat and shawl the moment we enter the hotel. Her march to the elevator makes her anger evident. I try to ignore it, but her attitude is filling up the elevator and I'm waiting for her to explode. Everyone is silent as we file into the elevator and I sense that all the men are trying not to look at the ticking time bomb.

"I don't know why we came here."

And so it begins. I exhale loudly at her outburst.

"You can't bring me to Rome and not take me to the Trevi Fountain. It's just wrong." She moves away from the back of the elevator and pushes her way up to me. I glance at her and hope she reads the warning in my eyes to stop.

"It's like taking me to a restaurant and not letting me order dessert."

The doors open and the men all disappear.

"Nate," I call him, and his shoulders tense but when he turns to me, his eyes are on fire.

"I don't get you," Maria shouts.

I grip her arm, cutting her off. "Stop it," I warn her.

My gaze flickers to Nate, his fist are clenched. "Stay with her in her room."

His eyes narrow, but he nods while opening his clenched fist. "Come on, Maria." His words are soft.

"No. I want you to explain to me what happened!" She's facing me now, demanding answers. Answers she deserves. Nate watches her, and his fondness for her is so obvious. I never noticed before. Maria is stunning looking, so all men look at her, but not with lust. Nate has something different in his eyes.

"One minute you're all normal and talking and the next you're like a bear on drugs." She's shaking her head and holds up her hands. "I want an explanation now." Her hands go to her hips and her brown eyes grow darker as she waits impatiently.

"You can see the fountain tomorrow."

"No. I don't ever want to see it." Her temper fires.

I shrug. "Fine." Giving Nate a nod, I turn away.

"I'm not finished, Damien." Her temper flares up and I'm glad I'm walking away from her. All I want to do is drag her into the room and make her mine completely.

CHAPTER NINE

MARIA

Nate tries to take my arm and I pull away from him. I'm too angry. I stomp to the room and I want to scream. I have no idea what I'm getting with Damien—his hot and cold personality is setting me off. He brings out the worst in me.

I want to throw myself onto the bed when I enter the room but I'm aware of Nate. I don't want him here, but he won't be allowed to leave.

"I'm sorry you have to babysit me," I say while dropping my hat and shawl on the chair. I open the balcony door and let some air in. It's hot outside. Nate doesn't answer and I glance over my shoulder at him.

"You okay?" He's so quiet and his eyes are troubled. Nate is fun. Seeing this side of him seems weird.

"Yeah." He forces a smile and my gaze skips to his fisted hands that he loosens. "He just pisses me off."

I'm startled at his level of hostility towards Damien. I wasn't under the impression that the two of them are friends, but he still works for Damien. Still, I can't blame Nate.

"Me and you both," I say.

His smile—this time—is real, and I see his shoulders relax. I root through the drawer and take out a pair of white shorts. The black maxi dress is too heavy. Grabbing a red strap top, I hold them up to Nate. "I'm going to get changed."

His nostrils flair and he nods while looking away from me.

The air is nice along my legs. The shorts cut off just under my ass and I grin when I think of Damien. I enter the bedroom and Nate is lying on the bed.

"Get off my bed," I say and he sits up, his eyes moving across my legs and then trailing up to my breasts. It normally never bothers me, but right now I feel exposed.

I'm tempted to get a light cardigan, but I tell myself I'm being stupid. Nate's seen me in a bathing suit loads of times. When I was younger, I used to wear the red set intentionally. It always set off my tan beautifully and the hungry eyes that followed me around the house used to fill up my ego.

I've never felt unsure about my body, so the feeling I'm having now is strange. I don't want the attention.

"Why are you frowning?" Nate sits up.

"Was I?" I try to relax my face.

"You could talk to your father." Nate gets off my bed and takes a step towards me. His eyes trail across my face. "Tell him how Damien treats you."

My stomach shifts uncomfortably. "He's my husband, Nate." My thumb touches the back of my wedding bands.

Nate stops walking. "That doesn't mean he can treat you badly." Nate's words are low and my heart slowly starts to pound. His eyes sear me and I hate what I see in them.

"Why are you looking at me like that?" He's never looked at me like this before. Why now? What changed?

"You deserve better." He looks away from me.

My hands grow clammy. "You think you're better?" I ask the question. I'm not dancing around this issue.

Nate's face grows hot, but he holds my gaze. "Yes."

I nod and my stomach twists. "That's never going to happen, Nate." He knows that. Even if I wasn't married to Damien, Nate and I would never happen.

"Don't go easy on me, Maria." He sounds hurt even as he tries to smile.

Would I have ever ended up with someone like him? He's sweet, and I could see him being caring. Nate's very handsome, but there isn't an attraction.

I sigh heavily. When I think of Damien, so much burns through my system. He makes me feel alive.

"I'm sorry. But trust me, you couldn't keep up with my demands." I grin. Nate smiles and I feel better. "So, are we good?"

"Yeah." He lies, but for the first time, I'm willing to accept lies.

"Are you hungry?" he asks.

I lie on my belly on my bed. "No." It's close to lunch time, but I don't feel like eating.

Nate grins at me as he reaches into his back pocket and takes out a deck of cards.

"You're carrying a deck of cards in your pocket?" I quiz, but I'm up on my knees. I love cards. It kept me occupied for hours on end when my dad or King kept me locked in the house.

"Found them at the bar last night." Nate starts to shuffle them and I don't believe him. I don't care where he got them from.

"What is it? Twenty Five? Snap?"

"Snap?" I question. Solitaire is my game.

He sits down on the bed as he continues to shuffle them. "Yeah. So we divide the deck and when the cards are the same..."

I cut him off, highly insulted. "I know how to play Snap."

He grins. "Prove it." He hands me half the deck.

I accept the challenge.

Nate starts and it's slow moving. "Is the deck rigged?" I get distracted and Nate roars. "Snap!"

I don't like losing. "Again."

He grins and gathers up the cards. We play another few games and I lose them all.

"You want a drink?" Nate asks while gathering all the cards up.

"Yeah, just a beer." Day drinking isn't my thing, but we're in Rome.

Nate hands me the cards and slides off the bed with a smile on his face. "Can I trust you?"

It's my turn to smile. "Absolutely not."

He goes to the mini bar and gets two beers. I try to match up a few cards, he's slow on purpose and when he returns, I'm ready.

We drink and play, and I lose another three rounds.

Nate boxes the cards again. "You want to play strip poker?"

I take a long drink while raising both eyebrows at him. "I've barely anything on." The drink is making me warm and fuzzy.

"I know." Nate's serious voice has me smiling at him.

"So, I'm at a clear disadvantage." I take another slow drink.

"I could take off my top?" He grips the hem of it.

I'm tempted to ogle all that tanned skin, but the sensible part of me kicks in. "No. You better not."

Nate grins. "You don't sound so sure." He raises his t-shirt a fraction and the hotel door opens.

The beer turns sour in my stomach when my eyes clash with Damien's. Nate can't pull his top down quickly enough without making us look guilty.

I want to tell Damien we were messing about, but his attitude earlier has me taking a long drink from my beer and getting off the bed. His jaw grows tighter as his gaze roams across me.

Nate gets off the bed and starts to slowly gather up the cards. I walk past Damien, the smell of his cologne has everything in me shifting.

He closes the door behind him as I place the empty bottle on the table and get another one.

"You want one, Nate?" I glance over my shoulder and Nate won't meet my eye. He's pocketing the cards.

"Nah." He's leaving.

"You don't have to go."

His eyes snap up to me before they bounce to Damien who still stands at the door. I'm not offering him a beer.

"No one said he had to." Damien speaks and steps deeper into the room, removing his suit jacket. My stomach tightens. His large shoulders and wide back make me remember clinging to them.

I try to clear my mind and look to Nate who's watching me while Damien's back is turned.

"I have some things to do." Nate makes his excuses. I could force him to stay, but the mood is ruined.

"What things?" Damien faces Nate.

"Work things." Nate answers him and bows his head while walking to the door.

"I didn't say you could leave." Nate stops.

I glare at Damien who steps closer to Nate.

"What were you doing last night?"

Nate frowns and shrugs. "Drinking at the bar. I wasn't working."

"The whole night?" Damien takes another step.

I tighten my hold on the bottle.

"If you want to ask me something, just ask me."

I applaud Nate's bravery. I'm all for the underdog.

Damien laughs, but it has no humor. "If I wanted to ask you something, I would. I prefer to extract the information my way."

I swallow at the threat in Damien's words.

"Check the cameras, I was at the bar." Nate tries to walk away but Damien strikes with his words.

"I did."

My heart pounds as my gaze bounces to Nate. What is going on?

I don't know what to do when Damien grabs Nate and drags him out to the balcony. I'm on his heels, my heart dancing in my chest.

"Damien." I warn, but he doesn't hear me.

"Where were you all night?" He shakes Nate like a rag doll before hanging him over the balcony.

"Damien, let him up."

Nate's face turns white as he looks behind him. "At the bar!" Nate's words are roared, setting off my panic.

"Damien! You let him up now, or I'm ringing my father." I'm afraid to touch him in case he lets Nate go. He has a savage look in his eyes as he stares at me. "Let him go." I repeat.

"Last chance. Where were you last night? Did you take the photos?"

Damien's anger rattles through Nate and I'm ready to throw up.

"I was in the city. At a brothel." Nate's words surprise me, but it's short lived as Damien drags him across the bar of the balcony. The minute he lets Nate go, his legs refuse to hold him up and he slides to the floor.

I'm beside him. "Are you okay?" I don't let him answer but stand and walk over to Damien.

He looks calm, and for the first time I see the man my father respects. My father always declared Damien as his right-hand man. I see why. He's vicious. My heart continues to pound and I'm shaking my head.

"Get out!" I roar at him.

He doesn't blink but stares at me like I'm an annoying fly. I may not have his strength, but that doesn't mean I won't fight.

"I said get out." My words are reduced in volume but carry more weight as he blinks.

He walks around me and drags Nate to his feet. My panic has me reaching for him. He's going to throw Nate over the balcony, my mind roars, but he pulls him through the double doors. I'm following them all the way to the bedroom door that he opens and pushes Nate out of.

Damien slams the door and I don't move.

I didn't want to be alone with him. I remain still as he turns to me and pulls off his tie.

He's going to tie me up. Through the fear comes my arousal and I take a step back from him. He passes me and enters the bathroom. I'm frozen as I watch him in the mirror. His shoes hit the floor heavily as he pulls them off. His feet are large as he removes his socks. I don't think he is giving me a strip tease, his anger has him not thinking.

His trousers hit the floor and the alcohol in my body has me zooming in on Damien's flesh. His legs are roped with muscles, even his ass looks solid. I can't see the front of him as he has his back to me. I'm sighing as I watch him. He's working on the buttons of his shirt. It slides from large shoulders and instantly I notice a difference in the texture of skin, the further it slips down the more horror fills me. His back is a canvas of pain. I inhale loudly and he turns, his chest a mass of chiseled muscles. But I can't let the image of his back go.

"What happened?" I tighten my arms around my waist. The puckered skin criss crossed his back.

My eyes want to trail downwards, but I hold his eyes.

"What are you wearing?" He fires back at me and takes a step into the room. I can't ignore his large erection.

I swallow as my eyes trail back up to him. "Clothes," I answer, too many clothes, I think.

"You have barely anything on you."

My heart pulsates. "I've more than you."

He pauses as if he remembers he's naked. "You won't be around Nate anymore."

My eyes keep drinking up all of him and it's too much. "No."

One word leaves my lips and he's closer. When did he move?

Fear worms its way through my veins. His eyes still shine with violence. He wouldn't hurt me, I tell myself, but I'm not convinced.

His grin has another wave of fear racing through me.

"No?" He questions. "Why was he taking his top off?"

Was that jealousy I saw or dominance? Did it matter?

"I told him I was at a disadvantage to play strip poker. So he suggested evening up the playing field."

"I bet he did." Damien growls.

My gaze drops low and my core tightens.

"He won't be around you anymore."

"That's not going to happen, you can't tell me who I can and can't see." My eyes move back up to his angry ones.

Wrong answer, his eyes ring. I don't know what I expect to happen, but it isn't his lips clashing with mine.

CHAPTER TEN

DAMIEN

I want to kill Nate, I would have thrown him over the balcony, but I wasn't sloppy in having witnesses. Especially when that witness is my wife, who is driving me mad.

She tastes of beer and everything I need to stay away from. Now isn't the time to touch her. Too much violence still roars through my blood. Her hands dig into my back, igniting painful memories. Everything melts together, the past and the present, and I grip her face. My cock throbs painfully for relief. She lands on the bed and I don't give her dazed eyes a second when I drag the tiny shorts off her.

I need to walk away. I need to stop this. My hands touch her long legs and when my fingers slip under her panties, I can't stop the primal need in me to taste her.

She groans as I suck the bunch of nerves that have her pushing her pussy up to meet my face.

Stretching her legs apart, I run my tongue along her pussy and down close to her ass. She's wet and I want to bury myself in every hole, to take what's mine.

After taking another taste of her pussy, I come up and let her taste herself. My cock rests close to her opening and I feel her tense under me.

She sucks my lips and when her hand wraps around my cock, I jerk at the surprise of her touch. Her eyes spring open, the brown swirls with desire. Gripping her hands I drag them back up to her head and hold them with one hand, she tries to object but when I plunge my finger into her pussy, she groans. Her tunnel wraps around me and I push another finger in. She's soaking and squirming under me. Her exposed neck screams for my belt and I move my fingers faster, not allowing myself to hurt her. Dragging my thumb back and forth over her clit, she jerks and thrashes until I know she's close to cumming. My cock throbs painfully, wanting its own release as she crashes and her own release pours across my fingers. I slow my movements before slowly taking my fingers out of her. She looks wild as she sits up and reaches for me. I slide off the bed and for the first time in my life expose my back to a woman. I've never allowed anyone to see it before. Maria doesn't stop me and I can picture the horror in her eyes. She won't follow me into the bathroom after seeing it.

"What happened?" She's on my heels and I shouldn't be surprised. I have to remind myself she isn't like the rest. That's why I want her more. I turn on the shower without looking at her.

"Why can't I touch you?" She fires another question.

I step into the shower and lather up my hands before facing Maria. Her eyes still swirl with desire, but it's not as strong as before. She's struggling not to look at my cock.

"Are you not satisfied? Do you want me to make you cum again?"

Her chest puffs up. She never put back on her shorts and her small red panties barely cover that sweet pussy.

"You're a bastard."

I laugh at her outburst and start to wash myself.

"I can see you want me, but why can't I touch you?" Frustration has her words falling from her swollen lips, but I can hear the vulnerable tone under her words.

I don't think I can simply cum; I want to bury myself in her while tightening my belt around her neck. I want to pound as deep as I can and take as much as possible.

Her hand goes to her hip in defiance and I've never wanted to break something so much.

"Come in here then." I offer.

She looks uncertain. Her top clears her head as she pulls it off. Her body is perfection. Her breasts bounce free as she unclips her bra and my erection grows tighter as she steps out of her panties. I don't blink as she comes into the shower. I know she's a virgin, so her confidence is a contradiction that makes me want her more.

"Get on your knees."

When she does, I tell myself to show some restraint, but it's hard with her looking up at me, while water drips down her breasts.

"Suck it." My heart races.

She leans in and doesn't hesitate. Her touch has me reaching for the tiles to balance myself. I groan as her small pink tongue flicks out and licks the head of my shaft. I'm tempted to push my cock down her throat, but I pull my mind as far back as I can and fight for restraint. I grip the tiles as she wraps her mouth around my cock and starts dragging it up and down.

"Oh, fuck." I open my eyes and look down at her, my cock jumps in her mouth as her eyes meet mine. I don't touch her. The temptation to grab her head and force her is almost overwhelming.

My body still moves to the rhythm of her movements. My cock hits the back of her throat and I feel her tighten around me. My hand leaves the tiles, ready to take, and I stop myself as she continues her painfully slow but tantalizing sucking. Her speed quickens and her hand joins her mouth.

I can feel the build up inside me, my excitement has me jerking as I look down at her. She's still watching me.

"I want you to drink it."

She takes her lips off my cock but her hand still strokes it, her movements are inexperienced but this is a first for me too, to allow anyone to have the upper hand.

She bobs her head, her eyes swimming with lust and this time when her warm lips wrap around my cock, she moves it quickly in and out of her mouth. Her fingers wrap around my balls and pull them. I push harder against the tiles, controlling the want to drag her off her knees and take her hard against the tiles. I close my eyes and cut off the want to allow the feel of her at my cock consume me, it doesn't take long before I can feel my climax approaching. I open my eyes and watch as she greedily takes my cock into her mouth. She's pulling harder at my balls and I jerk as waves crash through me and my cum sprays into her mouth. My hands leave the tiles and hold her head as I continue to jerk and empty myself in her. She slows her sucking and I can feel her mouth tighten as she swallows my cum before she licks my shaft clean. I can't take my eyes off her as she rises. Her confidence amazes me. She fills her hands with water and splashes her face, cleaning off some of the cum that she didn't capture. Once she's cleaned, she grins before stepping out of the shower. I have no idea what to make of her departure. I finish washing and when I enter the bedroom, she's dressed in a red maxi dress that clings to her curves. Straight away I want her to take it off and put on something less revealing.

She's brushing out her wet hair. Her brown eyes are soft as they trail across me and my stomach tightens.

"Will you tell me how your back got scared?"

I'm tempted to ignore her, but her determination wraps around her shoulders like a shawl.

"It was when I was a kid." I walk away from her haunted eyes and the memories that demand entry. Glancing over my shoulder and dropping my towel distracts her as I knew it would. But it's brief, she's focused on my back.

"Can I touch it?"

I freeze at her question. "No." I proceed to pull up my boxers.

Her face falls at my rejection. It's only skin. I tell myself.

"Does it still hurt?" Her words are measured and I know she won't give up.

"Touch it if you want."

She moves quickly across the room and each step has me growing more uncomfortable. I hold still as she moves behind me.

Her touch has me closing my eyes. The anger that bubbles up inside me isn't fair.

It's only skin, I remind myself, as her small fingers flitter across my past like she might be able to soften each blow.

"I'm so sorry, Damien." Her throat is clogged with tears.

I open my eyes. "It was a long time ago." I step away from her touch, because it may as well have been yesterday. I continue to get dressed without looking at Maria. She's watching me, her eyes are heavy on my back. The moment my suit is on, I ring Charlie.

"I need you to watch Maria."

"I'll be right there." Charlie speaks down the phone. I'm waiting for Maria to throw a strop at having Charlie watch over her, but her silence kills me as I leave the room without a second glance.

There aren't many people in the bar. "A whiskey," I order. The stool drags along the floor as I sit down and wait for the drink. The bartender tries to engage in conversation but I glare at him and he fucks off.

The whiskey burns, but it doesn't stop the anger that bubbles up inside me.

"Happy Birthday, William," I say, and his freckled face stretches wide. The excitement in his eyes was worth stealing the peach that I had wrapped up in an old newspaper. I took it from Father John's desk when he wasn't looking.

I shiver against the cold. It's five in the morning and our meeting has to be done in secret.

His eyes grow wide as he holds up the peach and my heart swells with pride.

"For me?"

I grin, my stomach rumbles wanting a bite. "Yeah, I just ate," I lie. The first bite has the juices running down his chin.

"Best birthday ever." His eyes dance with happiness and for the moment we were happy.

It was a flash of light in the darkness but even now, I can feel the cold of that morning, the crisp air that filled my lungs, the peach that filled my brother's mouth. My back aches with reflections of the memory. It's like seeing your face in the water, it shifts and moves but it's your face, just distorted, not real. I want it to disappear.

"Another." The bartender pours me another whiskey and it burns.

His eyelashes are so long, the wetness from his tears cling to them, making them darker. He lays on his belly while holding my hands and he cries. Even as blood pools around us, no one comes and he never left me, so I refuse to leave him.

I push on the empty glass when all I want to do is smash it.

Taking out my phone, I ring Terry. "Get us on the next flight home."

I've had enough of Rome and I need distance from Maria. I don't wait for Terry to answer me. I close the phone.

"Another." I call to the bartender as I try to drown the cries of my brother out.

CHAPTER ELEVEN

MARIA

I sit out on the balcony after Damien leaves. His departure makes me more determined to help him. He's running from whatever put those scars on his back and I want to help him. He said that the school he went to was run by violent priests. My heart hurts for a young Damien. Did they hurt him?

I try to take my mind off Damien and focus on the city in front of me. There is something majestic about being so close to the center of billions of people's world. Yet, the Pope is only a man. One man who rules over billions. My mind goes full circle back to the priests and Damien. To think of someone who has that power and abuses it. How young was he? I'm not even sure if it was a priest who hurt him, but it's a picture I'm forming in my head. The beauty of the city starts to dwindle and something sinister shadows the city.

Charlie walks past the balcony door but doesn't come out. I just need space from being constantly watched. I swallow. I can still taste Damien in my mouth. His cum was salty and thicker than I could have ever imagined. But it's Damien's ecstasy that coats my tongue and makes my body hum again.

The door in the bedroom opens and I'm leaving the balcony. The cold glass under my palm on the sliding door is what I focus on as I pause in the doorway. Damien's eyes are dark and coated in pain. My heart palpitates. He looks away from me and to Charlie.

"We are leaving in one hour." Charlie doesn't question Damien. It's a bob of his head and he leaves the hotel room.

"Why?" I step into the room and this time when Damien looks at me he's more closed off, he's more controlled. The pain is receding while dragging away any warmth that I had seen in his eyes before.

"You asked to see Rome and you got to see it." He's packing his bag while he speaks.

"I'm not done, yet." My words fall on deaf ears as he continues to pack. He's closing me off and I'm not going backward with him. I march over and pull his clothes out of the suitcase. He glares at me and I dump them on the floor without breaking eye contact.

"Maria." He growls while stepping away from me. He runs his hand across the light stubble that has started to appear across his jaw. The shadow looks good on him, but his tense frame has alarm bells ringing through my body and something is telling me to stop.

I ignore it. "No, Damien. I'm not done."

He glowers at me before bending down and picking his clothes off the floor. When he places them back in the suitcase, frustration tears through me.

"What did I do?" I lean in, trying to catch his eye. "Why am I being punished?" My voice rises.

He flickers me a glance before stuffing more clothes in his suitcase. "You're not. I have work."

My stomach twists. "You are a liar," I say it slowly.

He pauses and glares at me. "What do you want me to tell you?"

"The truth." I think I've finally gotten through to him.

He zips up the suitcase and grins. "I have work. We don't all get to do what we want all day."

His words sting. I don't get to do what I want at all. So his words are unfair.

"It's not always about you, Maria." His grin is still on his hard face.

He wants to hurt me.

I force a smile. "I scare you," I say while nodding.

His laughter is forced. "You are a pain in my ass."

I'm shaking my head. "No, I see it. I scare you. Maybe you like me and that scares you."

Something in his shoulders changes and he drags the suitcase off the bed and places it on the floor.

"I'm going to be frank here with you. What happened today won't happen again."

My stomach roils.

"It was a mistake. Now pack your stuff. We are leaving."

"A mistake? You don't just do those things by accident." My chest tightens. I've done things with him that I'd never done before.

"It was only foreplay." He turns his back on me and my heart squeezes.

Not to me, what we did was so much more. No one had ever rejected me, but this is worse. Damien is hurting me. It makes no sense. One minute we're making out and the next he wants nothing to do with me. Maybe this is how men really are? I want to scream at him, but he leaves the room with his suitcase. I'm tempted to sit here and put up a fight, but for the first time, I start to question what I am fighting for.

I drag my suitcase down to reception where everyone is waiting. No one speaks and it's a good thing because I think I'd chew them out. Charlie takes my bag and stows it in the trunk of the car. I mumble a thank you and get in. Nate won't look at me and neither will Damien. Jack gives me a smile and I don't return it.

Rome slips away as we return to the airport. With it I feel I'm leaving something precious behind.

The flight is leaving in five minutes and I'm grateful we don't have to hang around. I find myself seated in first class again—it's been reserved just for us. I pick a seat away from Damien. Right now he's giving off stay away vibes and I'm pissed with him, so I decide to listen.

I look up to find Nate watching me. I think of Damien's warning to stay away from him. My anger has me smiling at Nate. He smiles back.

"Are you okay?" I mouth the words slowly.

He nods. "Are you okay?" he mouths back.

I shrug and with my hand I rotate it back and forth like a rocking boat. To say it's touch and go. I stick out my tongue just to confuse the matter and he smiles.

Nate pulls a face and laughs silently. We are such children, but it's nice after so much tension. I had learned the sign language that said "Why don't you fuck off?" I do it to Nate and he narrows his eyes at me. I laugh but it's cut off when a brooding Damien blocks my view.

"You're in my way," I say as I try to look around his legs. He reaches in, his fingers wrap firmly around my wrists as he pulls me to my feet. I don't look at Nate as Damien walks me up the aisle. I like the feel of his fingers on my skin. We stop at the front seats and Damien makes me sit before sitting beside me. Charlie is across from me and won't meet my eyes.

"You can't seem to make up your mind," I say as I buckle my belt in. The seatbelt sign has come on over head. "One minute you want me, the next you don't." I refuse to look at him, but I'm angry and I'd like everyone to know why I'm so confused.

"Hot and cold," I place my hands in my lap. Charlie is buckled in and he's reading the manual about what to do in an emergency.

"Up and down," I add and I don't get a reaction.

"The award for the most indecisive person goes to Damien."

More silence.

"I don't think that will save you, Charlie." I focus on him instead and there is a moment of victory when his gaze rises but his head doesn't move. At least I know someone can hear me. Charlie turns the manual in his hands and reads the title.

"He wasn't reading it. You're just making him uncomfortable." Damien speaks with his eyes closed.

I glare at his side profile, the stubble suits him, it makes him look even more dangerous than he already does.

I turn to Charlie. "Am I making you uncomfortable, Charlie?" I smile sweetly at him.

"Of course not, Maria." Charlie says.

I glare at Damien. "See, it's not me."

Damien opens one eye. "He was hardly going to tell you the truth." I swear I see laughter in his eye.

I turn to Charlie. "Are you lying to me?"

Charlie won't meet my gaze as he folds the manual and puts it down on the empty seat next to him. He unbuckles his belt and stands. I watch him until he stops five rows back before he sits down and disappears.

"Now look what you did," I say to Damien as the flight attendant checks that we are all buckled in for take-off.

"No, that was all you, Maria." He looks at me now and my stomach quivers.

I have an overwhelming desire to hit him. "Maybe, but no matter what way you look at it, it's your fault."

His grin is small. "Anything else you would like to blame me for, Maria?"

The way he addresses me irritates the shit out of me. I want to say something that will cut to the bone.

"You're a sloppy kisser." I grin when I see Mattie and Jack smirk across the aisle. I feel proud. He's the best kisser, he's the only one I've ever kissed, but I want to embarrass him.

"Is that really the best you have?" Damien turns in his seat—facing me—and I'm starting to think I've bitten off more than I can chew.

The plane shifts and Damien closes his eyes and tenses.

"Are you afraid of flying?"

"Why, do you want to store that in your file to use against me?" His words are angry.

I hate it. I want to know everything about him because I'm falling for him.

He opens his eyes and I can see the fear in them. He's afraid of flying, the man who seems afraid of nothing. I have the urge to touch his face, so I

84

tighten my hands together in my lap. "I like you." I admit as the plane tears down the runway.

He blinks like he isn't sure he heard me right. I think I've surprised him and I lean back into the chair as the plane takes off into the air. "But most of the time you drive me crazy." I finish off and look at him. He's still staring at me.

When I smile at him he sits back in his seat. I think I've just rendered Damien speechless.

CHAPTER TWELVE

DAMIEN

I keep my eyes closed long after the plane is in the air. Maria is still beside me, her silence is heavier than her earlier words that she likes me. My heart jumps, but I need to remember I am her first for everything—and that can blur the lines easily. She has no idea of who I truly am. She likes an idea of me; she likes orgasming. I open my eyes and peek at her; she's staring out the window. I unclip my belt and feel her eyes on me instantly.

"Why are we going home?" Her question is spoken softly and I crave distance from her.

"I already told you." I met her eyes.

She shakes her head and looks away.

I get up and see Charlie a few rows back. The minute I sit beside him, he starts to apologize.

"I don't do well with the female species." Charlie's words are low.

I hold up a hand. "No explanation needed." He did what I wanted to do. I glance up now and Maria is staring daggers at me. I squash the amusement I always feel at her behavior. She isn't good for my system. I need to flush her out.

"I need you to do something for me." I glance sideways at Charlie.

The black leather jacket he wears tightens when he turns while bobbing his head.

"I need you to look into Maria. Just her past friends, school friends, anything that isn't right, let me know."

"No problem."

I glance up to find Maria not in her seat. She hasn't passed us, so she's still here.

"One second," I say to Charlie before standing up. Her legs peek out from the side of the seat. She's lying across the seats. I sit back down.

"When her father asked me to marry her, I had Andrew just take a quick look into her background to make sure nothing was amiss."

Charlie's jaw tightens and he can see where I am going with this. When Kane had offered Maria to me, I knew it was a deal that was too good. But soon he explained it was for her protection. I was just keeping her safe and getting paid to do it. I needed to make sure I wouldn't have some crazy ex-boyfriend stalking me, so I had Andrew do a background check. I didn't expect anything to come back since Maria was under constant lock and key.

"I think he found something, I think that's why he's dead," I say what I had feared from the moment he had been on my property. He wasn't supposed to be there that night. Was he coming with some information? I have no idea, but something isn't adding up.

"He hadn't been in work the day before." That day I won't forget, Maria had stomped into my office and took every business mind in the room to a dangerous place of pleasure with just her appearance.

"I need to retrace his steps and try to find out what happened."

"You think he found something?"

Maybe I'm overthinking it, but my instincts are what have allowed me to survive so long in this business.

"I'm not sure. I just want you to be careful and discreet. Don't tell anyone else."

"I'll get on it the moment we return." Charlie is loyal and I know I can trust him. Mattie and Jack are loyal to Kane, but Charlie would back me up if he had to pick. The others, I'm not so sure about.

I get up and pass Nate. He's another problem that needs to be solved. I glare at him from the corner of my eye and he fires back the same level of hostility.

Maria's asleep across three seats. Taking down a blanket from the overhead compartment, I place it across her sleeping form.

Her hands are joined together in prayer under her chin. Her wedding band sparkles. My own band feels heavy on my finger with the responsibility of keeping her safe. I knew she was going to be trouble, just not this amount of it.

I stay away from Maria for the rest of the flight and pick a seat away from everyone. The flight feels like it goes on forever until the food arrives. I take a coffee and salad and start to eat. I can sense her before she appears beside me. I try not to react.

"Why are you hiding?" I don't look up at Maria, but continue eating instead.

She doesn't leave.

"You're not sitting here." I glance at her standing in the aisle with a sandwich and tea in her hand. I push a warning into my voice—one that she completely ignores as she sits down beside me.

"You wouldn't pull down my tray for me, would you?"

She's holding her hands high while waiting and I can't just leave her waiting there. I lean across and pull down her tray.

"Thanks."

I grumble and return to my food. What would I have to do to make her go away?

"So, I was thinking of getting a job."

The salad is tasteless on my tongue as I chew. "No," I say around a mouthful of food. I have enough of a job keeping her safe while she's in the house. Maria having a job is another layer I'm not adding.

"Only part time."

I look up at Maria. She takes a bite of her sandwich as she waits for my answer.

"I said no. You don't need money, you have everything you want." She has no reason to work, ever.

"It's not about the money, Damien." She frowns and I'm tripping over how she says my name. It sounds good.

I remind myself that I need to keep my distance.

"I have so much time on my hands." She shrugs.

"Go do some shopping." I take a sip of coffee and nearly spill it as she throws down her sandwich and turns to me.

"What do I look like to you?"

"Keep your voice down." The whole plane is going to hear her going off on me.

"I want to do something valuable. I'm not some airhead."

Her cheeks darken with temper and I continue to eat my rabbit food. I can almost feel the heat radiate off her.

"You want me to spend your money?"

I look at her.

She raises a brow. "I can spend your money." She smiles now. "Expect a lot of deliveries when we get back."

I exhale loudly and want to respond, but instead, I finish my meal with her huffing and puffing beside me. She soon gathers up her half-eaten sandwich and tea and leaves me in peace.

It's not really peace, it's me playing the scene in the shower with her over and over again in my mind.

***

"Let's start this party!" King pulls me into him for a quick half hug. He is high on drugs, his eyes dance in his head as he releases me and downs a shot. I look around the club and see Gerald at the back of the room, his focus is on the girls who dance on stage. Gerald is the owner of the club and the man who got me into security. He's opened doors for me that I didn't know existed. I take a shot before patting King on the back.

"Be right back."

King is too focused on the dancers in front of him and nods without looking away from them.

"Gerald." I step up beside him.

"Boys night out?" He doesn't look away from the dancers.

"You can join us if you want." I know he won't, he rarely takes part and since he found Cara, he's being quieter than normal. If he's not working, he's with her, but joining in wasn't something he did anymore.

He shakes his head. "I've a busy night ahead of me."

King looks up at me and raises another shot. Three of his friends sit back and watch the dancers. This is code for a card game. When he invited me, I was going to say no again, but Maria is burning through my system and maybe this place will take my mind off her.

"Is Debbie available?" I don't look at Gerald; his eyes are heavy on me now. They wouldn't be filled with judgment. He did—after all—create this place.

"I'll sort it."

"Thanks." My stomach twists, but I need to get Maria out of my system.

So far, being in the office for the last three days didn't stop her from barging in and demanding more things. She wants a dog, she wants a job, now she wants to redecorate the kitchen. It's ridiculous. The house is brand new. She lived up to her promise of spending my money. Deliveries are arriving daily. The most recent purchase was an aquarium for fish we don't even have. It took three men to carry it into the house. Her face beamed with victory when I arrived home and saw what was going on.

I had sent Jack to mind her and keep her away from me, but the more time I was away from her, the more I thought about her.

I return to King, who hands me a shot. "To my brother." He raises his glass.

"I'm not your brother," I say before downing the shot. "What is that?" It's a mixture of everything and tastes so bad.

"Rocket fuel." King declares.

The more drink I take in, the more my body relaxes. King's friends don't drink as much as he does and I'm starting to think they aren't his friends, but bodyguards who have been paid to look like they are just part of the party.

I take another look at King and there is no doubt that he's very drunk. I glance around and finally I catch Gerald's eyes. He gives me a nod. King won't care that I'm with another woman, but I still don't want it known.

"Back in the minute." I tell them but they are all focused on a dancer on the stage. She's new here. I haven't seen her before.

I spot Candy on a smaller podium. She's been dancing here since I started. She winks at me as I walk past her.

Pushing the red curtains aside, I open the door and enter the hallway of the boom, boom rooms. The music disappears and there's an undercurrent of moans from behind the doors. Each door has a small opening that allows you to see in. I pass all the doors and stop at the opened one at the end.

Debbie is setting out a row of toys and when she spots me, she smiles. "Hello, sexy."

I close the door behind me and remove my suit jacket.

She picks up a belt from the row and snaps it. "I have your favorite."

It's been weeks since I've been here, a week before I married Maria, to be precise. But this place that used to be my playground feels different now.

Debbie's in a black thong and red heels. That's it. That's all I ever want. She ties her hair up as I remove my tie.

"You need a hand?" Debbie moves over to me, she knows not to touch unless I allow it.

"No!"

She narrows her eyes at my sharpness.

I need to do this. I need to escape back into what I know. My tie joins my suit jacket on the chair. I take everything off except my shirt. When I turn to Debbie, she is ready. She hands me the belt and I feel my erection grow as I wrap my fingers around the leather.

CHAPTER THIRTEEN

MARIA

I know Charlie is watching me. I can feel his heavy eyes on my back.

"To the left." I tilt my head and create a square with my fingers that I look through like a camera.

"Here?"

I grin. "Perfect."

The three guys look at each other before looking back at me. I have the aquarium set up in the hallway. There is enough space to slide in either side to get into the house. But it's a tight squeeze for larger people. Damien in particular.

"You can leave through the back door," I tell the delivery men as I stare at it. He can't ignore the monstrosity in the hallway, I'm not sure how long I can look at it.

I glance over my shoulder at Charlie. He's watching me with a serious expression. His jaw is set, not in anger. He was born like that.

"What do you think, Charlie?" I smile.

His eyes jump away from me. "Very nice, Maria."

It's not nice at all. "Where is Andrew?" I like Andrew, at least he entertains me. This time when I glance over at Charlie, his expression has my stomach squeezing. It's not a look he wears often. I know before he even speaks that something bad has happened.

"Andrew passed away, Maria." He frowns, and steps away from the wall that he's been leaning against the last hour while I got the men to drag the aquarium around the hall.

"What happened?" He was too young to be ill. My mind jumps from a car accident to sudden death.

Charlie's frown deepens and he scratches his forehead before leaning back against the wall. "I'm not sure."

I raise a brow. "You don't know how your friend died?"

"We were not friends. I didn't know him." Charlie's Russian accent is peeking out between the curtains of his emotions.

I let it go and face my aquarium, I need to get fish. I need to fill it with water. Maybe I can get some tropical ones.

"Can you fill the aquarium for me, Charlie?" I ask without looking at him. My eyes skip to the silent front door. Where is Damien? I can feel the hands of time tighten around my throat. I don't want to become that woman that sits watching a closed door, thinking any second it would open. I don't want that. I don't want to be my mother. Yet, here I am.

My mother gave her youth and beauty to my father, and in my opinion, she didn't get much back. I drag my mind away from her; it isn't a place I want to go. A person I refuse to become. I turn on my heel and enter the kitchen as Charlie comes out with a large basin of water. He'll be here all night.

We have all night. A voice whispers. I refuse to listen to it as I march out into the back garden that's still being landscaped. Across the half-built wall that will surround the patio area, I see the yellow hose that I spotted before. Picking it all up, I drag it back into the house.

"Charlie." I call as I hoist it to the sink. He steps back into the kitchen and places the basin on the counter.

"Thought this might help." I grin, feeling proud.

Charlie doesn't react but hooks the hose up to the sink before unraveling it and bringing it to the aquarium.

"Turn on the tap." Charlie calls and I do. The hose swells as water rushes through it, I hear it hit the bottom of the tank.

Charlie stands holding the hose and my mind trails back to Andrew. "I don't like lies." I say to the water. "I can tolerate so many things, like I appreciate when someone tells me, they just can't tell me, or they tell me they don't want to tell me. I like a reason no matter what. As long as that reason is true. But I don't like lies." I glance at Charlie. He's also staring into the tank. "What happened to Andrew?"

"You should ask Damien."

I nod, accepting his answer. He isn't allowed to tell me. I'm ready to thank him for being honest when the front door opens. The slam of the door has my blood roaring to life. I watch Damien's legs waver as water fills the tank. His eyes drink in the tank.

"What are you doing?" He frowns as he steps up to the tank.

He looks disheveled. My stomach hollows and I'm moving. I slide along the side of the tank until I can see Damien fully. My gaze roams across him, ticking off all the oddities. No tie, top button of his shirt open.

I step closer to him. "Is that perfume?" I want to question him immediately about Andrew, but my question dies and shrivels as I inhale the smell of cheap perfume.

"New aftershave." He lies so easily and his eyes hold no remorse.

I don't expect the assault on my system. I'm not ready to care this much about him, about us.

My heart pounds in my chest as I speak. "Don't lie to me." I can handle a lot of things, but not lies.

"You really fit the role of the wife." Damien moves away, trying to end this conversation.

I block him. "Why do I smell perfume off you? Who were you with?" Heat scorches my cheeks and anger tightens my fists.

"I wasn't with anyone." His growl is said inches from my face. A part of me believes his words, but my senses know what they smell—and that's perfume.

"What is that in my hall?" He points at the aquarium and I turn to it. Charlie is focused on the water as it continues to fill. It doesn't feel like a victory anymore. It looks like a wife that has too much time on her hands.

I swing back to Damien, his eyes roam across my face. "Who were you with?" The moment the question is out of my mouth, he walks around me and up the stairs. My heart pounds harder.

"Go home, Charlie." I shout without looking at him. I stand and wait until the water stops running and the back door closes before I follow Damien upstairs.

"I didn't sign up for this." I'm marching up the stairs, my brain is telling me to calm down and just get even, but my heart won't settle.

Pushing open his room door, he glares at me.

Separate rooms.

"I didn't sign up to have a cheating husband."

He clears the space between us as he pulls off his suit jacket and flings it on his bed. His face grows deadly close to mine. "I wasn't with anyone."

"Liar." I shout, my temper flaring. "I can smell her perfume." There, I've slammed an identity on her.

He's making me second guess myself with how honest he looks, but I know what I smell.

He scrubs his hands across his face and steps back from me. "I was out with King, having a few drinks."

I laugh. "Is that supposed to make me feel better?" I walk deeper into his room, my eyes want to move across all his possessions and learn what makes up Damien. "You think I'm buying the whole I was with your family crap." My hand collides with his chest. "You think I'm that dumb?" I push him again and he stumbles back. It's not enough. I strike out again when he doesn't answer me.

His large hands capture mine and he yanks me into his chest. "I told you I wasn't with anyone. I didn't lie." His words ring true again.

I'm staring up into the vortex of green that's sucking me in. My body is aware of everywhere we touch. I hate how aware of him I am.

His eyes flicker across my face. "I was considering it."

His words have me pulling away from him. My stomach twists and I step away.

"But I didn't." He finishes.

"Should I be thanking you?" More words fall flat. That's how I feel right now, flat. "Should I be grateful?" He won't look at me now. "Two weeks in and my husband hasn't cheated, but he has thought about it. He's thought about it so much, that he smells of cheap perfume."

"Stop it, Maria." His growl would normally warn me that I'm stepping into uncharted territory, but from the day I married him, I've been out of my depths.

"I hope she was worth it." I turn on my heel and march from his room. I won't stand there and beg. Tears blur my eyes as I step away. I hear him behind me and a small part of me blossoms, it's short lived as his belt tightens around my throat and I can't breathe.

He's strangling me.

CHAPTER FOURTEEN

DAMIEN

She's struggling and panicking. Her hand swings back and she tries to claw at me.

"Maria, trust me." I loosen my hold on the belt, giving her some room to breathe. It's a small window. My erection brushes painfully against my trousers.

"I need you to trust me." I repeat and she stops fighting and finally takes in some air. I run my hand along her side.

"Take it off me, now." She's fighting for control. Her voice is too high pitched.

I drag her body closer to mine and she stiffens when my erection brushes up against her tight ass.

"I wasn't with anyone," I whisper the words into her ear while brushing her hair that's gotten caught up in the belt aside. The belt feels perfect in my hands; it feels even more perfect around her neck.

"I have a certain taste." She's so still in my arms. Her hands hang on either side of her body. She's stopped fighting. I keep the belt around her throat but lessen my hold. "I like the control." I press a kiss to her jaw.

"I want to take you from behind." Her chest starts to pump harder and I place another kiss on her jaw.

"I want to bury my cock inside you, Maria." She tries to look at me, but I tighten the belt around her neck.

"I want to fuck you hard." Her body responds by falling into me and my cock twitches. "I want to fill your tight pussy and hear you scream."

My hand grips the belt as I let the other roam across her body. My hand dips into her waist band.

"Do you want me?" I push her panties aside and dip my finger inside her wet pussy. I smile into her neck. "You're wet."

A virgin.

I shouldn't be touching her. I pull my hand up and hers clamps over mine, stopping me.

"Touch me." Her words are whispered with desire and I have no will power left. I push my finger back inside her and let her juices coat my fingers. She wiggles, pushing her ass closer to my throbbing cock.

"I want to bury myself in you," I whisper as I push a second finger into her. She exhales loudly.

I don't think if I had been with Debbie, that it would ever dampen my desire that I feel for Maria. Debbie had been ready and all I could see was big brown eyes questioning me.

I pull my hand out of Maria and release her. She stumbles from my hold and immediately her hands goes to her red neck. My cock twitches again.

"I want this." Maria's wide brown eyes hold mine.

I should say no. I should walk away. I wasn't supposed to touch her.

"You have to trust me."

She nods eagerly and it reminds me of her innocence that's wrapped up in all that confidence.

"Take off your clothes." She hesitates but starts to strip. I tighten my hold on the belt until she stands in only her black bra and underwear.

"All of it." I remove the belt from her neck.

She hesitates again and I think she's reconsidering until she pushes her panties down and steps out of them while working on her bra. I kick off my shoes without looking away from her perfect body that I want to fuck so badly.

"Turn around." She spins, her eyes clouded with desire. I remove my trousers and let my cock spring free from my boxers. I stroke it as I walk to Maria. She inhales as I push my bare cock up against her ass.

"You want me to fuck you in there?" I ask. I want to claim every hole.

"Yes." She's breathing heavy. Her nipples are rock hard as I run my thumb across them before lowering my hand to her sweet pussy. She's dripping and I wet two fingers before sliding them back out and bringing them to her mouth.

"Taste it." I command. Her pink tongue flicks out and wraps itself around my fingers. My cock pushes against her ass, demanding entry.

I run my other hand that still clutches the belt in between her legs. She exhales loudly at the contact of the cold buckle against her clit. I move it across the bunch of nerves as I dip a finger inside her. Her walls clench around my finger. She's still sucking and licking my other hand, and my cock feels ready to explode against her ass.

"Get on your knees." I stand back and she immediately goes to her knees. "Hold on to the banister." Her tanned hands wrap around the white banister as she kneels down.

She is so fucking perfect.

"Spread your legs." She does and I love how responsive her body is to me. I dip two fingers in again, going as deep as she will allow before dragging her juices back up. Rubbing the liquid on her ass, my cock hardens painfully. I reach down and stroke it before placing it at Maria's pussy.

"Come up to me." Maria lets the banister go and moves until her back is flush with my chest. I place the belt around her neck.

"You have to trust me," I say before kissing her jaw.

She looks at me from the corner of her eye. Desire swims in the depths of brown along with fear. "I trust you."

I smile at her before kissing her harshly. "Hold on to the banister." She does and I keep my hold on the belt that I tighten around her neck.

I push two fingers into her pussy before adding a third. Moving my hands quicker in and out of her, I pull on the belt and her juices coat my fingers quickly. My own need to be inside her has me removing my fingers and putting the tip of my cock in her opening. Her body freezes under me and she tries to turn around.

"Take off your shirt." Her command is strangled. The determination in her eyes has me ripping the buttons with one hand and pulling it from my back. I push my cock in and she cries out, facing forward.

I should be gentle but my body is demanding that I fuck her hard and take what I want. My thumb slides across her ass and she tightens around my cock. I push it in deeper before taking it out. I continue to play with her ass until she loosens around my hard cock. I'm barely in and all I want to do is fuck her roughly.

I tighten my hold on the belt, forcing her head back to me as I push into her. She cries out, her hands reaching for the belt.

"Keep your hands on the banister."

She re-wraps her hands around it as I push deeper before pulling out. I'm struggling to control my pace as I yank harder on the belt. My thumb dips into her wet ass and I push deeper until my cock is consumed by her pussy. She's so tight. I pull out and I can't slow as I slam back into her, my thumb sinks deeper into her ass. Her hands are gripping the banister and I push in again before pulling out quicker. I move faster, my body demanding I take my pound of flesh. She's so fucking tight.

I yank the belt again, pulling her further back and I hear her strangled cry. I slam my cock into her pussy and I don't want her to come yet. Removing my cock is agony when all it wants is to be inside her. I keep my thumb on the outside of her ass, as I lessen my hold of the belt. I don't let her move but put three fingers inside her pussy.

She's breathing heavy as she looks at me over a shoulder, her eyes are wild with desire as I plunge three fingers into her pussy.

"Come up to me." She moves instantly ready to listen to my commands. She's eager as I place my hand over her mouth.

"Taste yourself." Her tongue flicks across all my soaked fingers. My cock prods against her ass and I move it to the opening and push in.

She exhales loudly and when she pushes her ass against my cock, my restraint slips. I remove my fingers from her greedy mouth and without telling her, she bends over and grips the banister. My cock slides into her pussy easier this time and when I withdraw, I tighten the belt around her neck before slamming back into her.

I hold back as I move in and out of her at a steady rhythm. I return to playing with her ass until it consumes my finger easily. I want to fuck it. My movements quicken and I yank her back as I bury my cock in her. "Come for me." I command her as I start to pump faster and harder into her pussy. My flesh slaps against hers and I ride her faster and harder. She's moaning and gasping. Her hands tighten on the banister as I pound into her, not able to hold back, not able to stop. I feel my release coming quickly and I pummel her pussy until my seed pours inside her. I jerk and let it spill, I sense her tightening around my cock and I loosen my hold on the belt as she comes across my shaft. I jerk and move in and out of her until I'm completely empty. Sweat makes a pathway down my back.

Maria tightens around my cock and I move it slowly out of her. My cum drags along too and it's so fucking perfect to see it spill from her pussy.

I release the belt from her neck. She still grips the banister as she catches her breath. For the first time I'm aware of how stiff she is.

"Are you okay?" Fear clutches me. She was a virgin and I didn't go easy.

"I'm not sure." She answers.

I feel like an animal. I make her look at me.

The beast in me settles as she smiles. "That was..."

Her cheeks are flushed and she's never looked so innocent. I kiss her mouth softly and can taste her juices.

"Are you okay?" I ask again as I soak up the look of awe and shock in her eyes.

She nods. "I think so."

She's so perfect. I run my fingers across her red neck. "You need to get something on that before it swells."

105

She nods and rubs her neck. Getting up, I bring her into my bathroom. My cock twitches when she walks stiffly. She looks sore and I want to fuck her all over again.

I run the washcloth under the cold tap before squeezing it out. She takes it from my outstretched hand and pushes it against her neck.

"Next time I should wear a scarf," she says, looking up at me with astonishment in her eyes.

My stomach quivers at the words next time. It shouldn't have happened at all, but my cock continues to grow at her words.

"Let me get dressed." I leave her in the bathroom as I pull on a clean pair of boxers and trousers. It's odd to feel the air on my back with her so close. I have no idea why she wanted my shirt off, but I would have peeled my skin from my body just to fuck her.

I pull a t-shirt over my head before I re-enter the bathroom. She's still nursing her neck. She's sitting naked and cross-legged on the toilet and the smile on her lips is perfect.

"You enjoyed that?" I tease.

She smiles. "Just a little."

I laugh. "Hmmm." Taking the cloth from her, I run it again under the cold tap before squeezing it and handing it back to her. Maybe I got a little too excited with the belt.

"You'll have to wear a scarf for a few days," I tell her.

She stands up and looks at her neck in the mirror. A part of me cringes at how red it is.

She smiles. "You marked me." Her eyes clash with mine in the mirror, and the depths of joy in Maria's words make me wonder about the person that lies just under the surface.

"Why did you agree to this marriage?" My question has her facing me.

"Money." She answers while pushing the cloth against her neck.

"You already had money." I state as we leave the bathroom. I take out a dressing gown that she must have bought for me when we moved in. I've never worn it. She takes it and wraps it around her body before walking over to my bed and sitting down. There isn't the awkwardness that I often experience after sex.

She sits cross-legged and pulls her hair to the side before pressing the cloth against her neck. I lean against the dressing table and watch her.

She shrugs and frowns. "I suppose I did. It was about freedom too."

"You didn't get much freedom did you?"

She looks up at me. "No. But I got other things." Her smile grows on her lips.

"Did you have a happy childhood?" Her eyes drop to the bed and she removes the cloth from her neck.

"Why do you ask?"

She isn't someone who dodges questions, so I'm watching her more closely now.

"Why are you not answering?" I stand up straighter.

"What happened to your back?" She fires back at me.

I tighten my fists. "Are you hiding something Maria?" I step towards her and she holds still, there is no fear in her eyes.

I had Charlie look into her, and I now know what Andrew found out about her. It cost him his life.

Does she know?

She doesn't shy away from me.

"No. Are you?" She raises a perfect dark brow and I join her on the bed. I want to touch her neck again, but instead I push the fabric of the nightgown aside and reach for her pussy.

"You want me?" I ask as I slide a finger into her swollen pussy.

Her eyes are consumed with lust and I think I just may get my answer.

She isn't Kane's daughter. She isn't King's sister. I have no idea who she is.

CHAPTER FIFTEEN

MARIA

I'm so sore, but I don't want him to stop. "You like that?" I look into Damien's angry eyes. I have no idea why he's angry, and fear skitters along my spine, entwining itself with the pleasure that is spreading across my flesh. My nipples brush against the silky fabric of the dressing gown.

I want to lie back, but his hand curls into my hair and he holds me still as he continues to plow his fingers inside me. I want him in me but I don't move, his hold is restricting and the feral look in his eyes has my fear blossoming. It's like I'm not watching Damien. I close my eyes and enjoy the assault on my body that his fingers are producing.

"Look at me." His command has my eyes springing open. His hand tightens in my hair and I want this to stop, but the pleasure wins out as his thumb strokes the bunch of nerves at my opening. It doesn't take long for me to cum on his hand. The aftershocks have me riding his fingers. He's smiling when I come down and my surroundings register with me. What is he doing to me? I have no idea that this is what it would feel like. I've never felt so alive.

"If I ever find out you are lying to me..." He trails off and my brain is trying to catch up with his angry eyes. What did I miss? Why is he threatening me?

"What are you talking about?" My body still hums from my release. His hand snakes out of my hair and he's off the bed. Damien composes himself, but I see it's forced.

He's staring at me like he's piecing together a puzzle. "Nothing." He shakes his head. This is the first time I feel awkward. I wrap the nightgown around my body. I have no idea what hour it is at night, but I'm all for getting into bed. Damien is still standing and he looks torn. I have no idea what's going on inside his mind.

"I think we should get some rest."

I laugh at his serious tone. "Are you getting awkward because we had sex?"

His smile is quick and I see Damien again. "I can't figure you out," he says before his smile dissolves. "I don't like sharing my bed."

I don't get him at first, but the longer he stands looking at me the more his words sink in.

"Are you kicking me out?" Horror fills me.

"You have your own room." He stuffs his hand in his pockets.

I slide off the bed. "I thought when you have sex with someone, sleeping next to them would happen?" I can feel the heat in my cheeks. A part of me is pleading not to beg, but I can't just accept this and say nothing.

"I never do."

His answer cuts deep. Not even with me. I'm no exception.

"You should shower, I can still smell her perfume on you." My eyes burn as I leave his room with my head high.

My room appears cold, I have a sudden urge to mess up the perfectly made bed. My body still burns and my neck feels stiff. I don't move from the door as my mind buzzes with the horrible thoughts that I have turned into my mother. She would forgive and stay quiet, letting the storm pass.

I won't. I refuse to be silent. I slam my bedroom door and promise myself, for now, I will allow this...but Damien will pay.

With the morning comes clarity and I'm up early and in the shower. I've barely slept, my mind has jumped from what I did with Damien to how he dismissed me after. My core throbs—I wasn't prepared for this kind of pain. Once I'm dressed in a black leather skirt and my see-through black shirt, I spend some time on my makeup and fluffing my hair; the end result I smile at. I'm not going to blend into the background.

Charlie is in the kitchen when I arrive downstairs. He greets me like every morning and I give him a wide smile. "Good morning, Charlie."

I'd say he looks suspicious of my chirpy voice, but with Charlie he has the same serious face as usual. Pulling off a sticky note, I scrawl a message for the cleaner.

Do not wash Damien's clothes. I press it onto the fridge where she will check for notes. It was small, it was petty, but soon he would run out.

I pour out a bowl of cereal, and eat it, while Charlie reads a paper.

"We have some shopping to do today," I say.

Charlie glances at me over the paper before carefully folding it and setting it down. "That's no problem, Maria."

"Ring Nate, I'd like him along with us."

Charlie pauses. "I promise I can keep you perfectly safe."

I finish the cereal. "Keeping me safe or making sure I don't do anything that might be fun?" I get up, not expecting Charlie to answer me, and he doesn't.

"We are having a party tonight for Damien, invite everyone he knows." I smile over my shoulder at Charlie. He nods while taking out his phone.

"I expect Nate here in the next thirty minutes."

I leave the kitchen and finish getting ready, grabbing my bag and jacket. I return downstairs when the door opens, and it's not Nate, but King.

"I'm just heading out," I say as I clear the last step. He frowns at the aquarium before his focus returns to me.

"I heard you are having a party."

I glare in the direction of the kitchen. "It's for Damien."

King's eyes assess me. "Is it his birthday?"

I narrow my eyes at my brother. "King, does it matter? Now I'm not allowed to have a party?"

His laugh is quick and he walks to me and slings his arm across my shoulder while steering me into the kitchen. He doesn't get far as he stops at the aquarium.

"You want to tell me why this is here?"

Staring at it, I thought about how pitiful it would sound if I told him I did it to get a reaction out of my husband.

I glance at King, who watches me. I have no one else to talk to, but talking to King about Damien just seems wrong.

"It was a moment of anger." I shrug like it's no big deal.

"Are you in there Charlie?"

Charlie's disorientated image appears through the aquarium.

"You didn't fit along here?" King asks him from the side.

"I've been using the back door." Charlie admits.

I feel a bit bad that I've inconvenienced everyone.

"If you want to have a party, this has got to go." King says and I kind of like the aquarium.

"Damien bought it for me." I stare at it, like it was a gift. It was his money that purchased it. The tank cost him five thousand.

"Okay, bin it." I smile up at King and he has a look of victory in his eyes.

"So you want to have a party?"

I smile widely. "Can you invite everyone you know?" The sad truth is—I have no friends.

"Yeah, it's short notice but I'm sure we can pull it off."

"Damien will be so happy." I can't stop the smile that grows on my face. "I want this to be perfect. Do you know his friends and family?"

"I'll see what I can do."

"Thanks." I plant a kiss on King's cheek before calling Charlie.

"Did you ring Nate?"

"He will be here soon." Charlie speaks from the kitchen.

"I'll meet you in the garage." I call to Charlie.

"Can you get people to move my fish tank?" I say to King as we walk to the door.

"Anything else?" His brow rises.

I grin. "Nope, that's it."

"I'll sort it." King waves to Charlie before getting into his car. As King leaves, Nate pulls up and I give him a wide smile that he doesn't return.

"What's wrong?" I ask as he climbs out of his car.

He locks his car and walks past me. "Nothing." He mumbles before climbing into the back of the car.

I slide in the passenger seat and Charlie waits until I've buckled my belt.

Pulling down the visor, I try to find Nate in the back but I can't see him. He's sitting directly behind me.

"I hope you don't mind," I say to Nate as Charlie starts to drive.

"No, I don't." Nate speaks on an exhale.

"So, I'm having a party for Damien." I smile out the window as we pass a row of houses.

"He's not happy." Nate offers up and Charlie glances at him in the rear-view mirror. My cheeks hurt from smiling.

"Oh, no," I say in mock horror, and sense Charlie glancing at me.

Nate shuffles in the seat so he's more centered and I can see him when I glance over my shoulder now.

"What are you doing?" Nate asks.

I shrug innocently. "Nothing. Just giving my husband a party."

Nate narrows his eyes at me, but I see the amusement in them.

"He likes to party." I add and glance at Nate, who's looking at Charlie in the mirror. I don't know what passes between the men, but Nate sits back with a face on him.

We arrive at the mall and I don't waste a second filling up baskets with stuff. Charlie and Nate both push the trolleys that I fill. Half-way through, I feel so far out of my depth that I'm starting to question my decision.

"I miss Andrew." I say and glance at Nate. "His family must be devastated."

Nate's face pales and he nods. "Yeah, it was a shock."

I nod and pause at the aisle with household cleaning products. I stretch for the top product but can't reach it, I know I'm showing a lot of leg and when I glance at Nate, he's drinking me in.

"Can you get it for me?" I ask.

He's beside me. I take a quick peek for Charlie. He's across the way reading the label on some product. I return my focus to Nate as he hands me the can. I rotate the bottle to read the label. Starch for the perfect shirts.

"Damien hates when his collars don't stand up," I say before slipping the starch into the basket. "So sudden." I add.

Nate's eyes are focused on my chest and I hate the urge I get to fold my arms across my chest, but I remind myself this is what I want.

"Andrew's death," I remind Nate, trying to pull his head out of his ass.

"I thought it would be fine." He shrugs and his eyes slowly travel up to mine. "It hit his kidney, that's what caused him to bleed out."

My heart pounds when Charlie puts the product down. What the hell would hit someone's kidney?

"The bullet?" I ask, sounding absolutely ridiculous. This wasn't the wild west.

Nate looks at me again. "No, a knife."

"Andrew was stabbed?" My legs grow weak.

Nate looks to Charlie who joins us and it's so painfully slow when Nate realizes his mistake.

"I'm not sure." Nate tries to recover.

"You're not sure if he got stabbed and died?"

Nate looks to Charlie. "I thought she knew."

Charlie pushes the trolley forward and says nothing.

"You can't trick me like that, Maria." Nate sounds pissed, but I didn't expect to hear that something like that happened to Andrew.

"Why? Do they know who did it?"

Nate steps away from me, pushing the trolley. My mind moves in so many directions. I have no idea why someone would hurt Andrew. Was it a late night brawl? I've heard of those things happening.

I catch up with Nate. "You have to tell me what happened."

"No, he doesn't." Charlie cuts in and glances around him before dragging his trolley back to me. I recoil from his angry face. "We are here to help you with your party. That's it. No more questions."

I nod at Charlie and he looks like he just won. But the fact he doesn't want me asking questions, makes me more determined to figure out what happened to Andrew. They are hiding something from me and I am going to find out.

CHAPTER SIXTEEN

DAMIEN

I can't take my mind off Maria. I barely slept, knowing how close she was to me. All I wanted to do was slip into her room last night and fuck her. I shift the bulge that is growing just thinking of her.

Charlie rang earlier, informing me that she was throwing a party for me. She demanded Nate as well. I warned the little bastard to keep his distance, but I don't need Maria stomping in here if she doesn't get what she wants, so I let Nate go.

A knock on my office door has me taking the file on Maria, along with all the images, and sliding them into the top drawer on my desk. I look up as King walks in.

"Is it your birthday?" He asks with a grin. I can't help but look at King differently. I wonder, was he deceived into believing that Maria is his sister, or is he deceiving me? The main question is why?

"I hear we are having a party." I try to keep any suspicion hidden from him. King sits down and leans back in the chair.

"What did you do?" His voice is light like normal, but I can sense an undercurrent. Is he being more protective of her than normal?

"It's your fault for taking me out for drinks." I grin at him.

His scarred lip tugs up. "I saw you going behind the red curtain last night."

I didn't think he was aware; I had thought he was high. King might be far more aware than I have given him credit for. Maybe he's been placed here to watch me. Maybe all these visits will add up to something.

"She doesn't know." I answer quickly.

His eyes widened. "Good, if she did, I'm sure she'd have your balls cut off." His laugh is quick. I'm questioning what brother would sit here and be fine if I cheated on his sister.

"I thought maybe that's what had her throwing a party for you."

"Should I be scared?" I ask King.

He laughs again. "Nah, I pity Nate and Charlie today." King pulls his leg up across the other one. "So what happened behind the red curtain?"

His laughter is gone.

I'm weighing my words. "Same as what happens in any other brothel."

He nods while observing me. "But it's a little darker back there?"

"Why don't you try it sometime?" I offer up.

He grins again. "I'm glad you're getting it somewhere."

I sit forward in my chair and grin at him. "How do you know I'm not getting it at home?"

He's sitting forward too, and I see the warning flash in his eyes. "She's off limits, you know that."

I laugh and lean back in the chair. "I was joking. I know. I just didn't know you had seen my contract."

King still hasn't relaxed. "He'll have your head for it, if you do."

I drop the smile. "Him or you?" My heart pounds as King's eyes widen. He fucking knows she's not his sister.

"Both." He answers.

I nod while sitting back and trying to relax. "I'm curious, why is she off limits?"

"Have you ever heard the phrase on a need to know basis?" King asks while rising out of the chair.

I nod and tighten my jaw.

"You're on a need to know basis." His smile doesn't return. I've pissed him off. "See you tonight at the party. Don't be fucking late." He leaves abruptly.

I curse myself for showing my hand. He will watch me more now.

I take out the file and go over the information that Andrew had managed to get. His work was impeccable. Andrew had researched as much as possible.

My stomach twists as I hold up Maria's birth certificate. Andrew had followed the paper trail back to a guy who forged documents. Why had Kane gone to such lengths to hide Maria? Does Maria know? She acted odd yesterday when I had questioned her about her childhood. King knows something too. Andrew's research doesn't reveal who she is. The only thing he has circled is a second name that I type into Google now.

O'Brien. It comes up with a list of wineries, cafes, and alcohol. I exhale before taking out the photos again of Maria and me on the balcony in

Rome. Someone had followed us, or the person was already with us. Mattie, Charlie, Nate or Jack. I have to rule out Nate. His story was true, he had been at a brothel. I need to question Mattie and Jack. Charlie won't have. He has no need.

I close the file and push it back into the top drawer in my desk. I need to organize new guys for some security contracts I recently signed. My business is starting to lift off, but my time lately is consumed with Maria. I glance at my watch, I have a few hours before her party starts. I'm not going to be late. I don't want to piss King off anymore than I already have.

The gates to the house are already opened to accommodate the cars that park along the drive. My stomach tightens. I know she's mad, but now as I see the house lit up, I wonder how mad she really is—and what exactly I am stepping into. I pull up at the steps; it seems to be the only available space. Knocking off the car, I take a final look at my phone before getting out. The music is loud and the voices crawl over the beats as I enter the hall. I'm met by nods and smiles. I don't know these people. The main living space has been emptied and the room is full. In the middle of them all, is Maria, laughing and smiling while holding a flute of champagne. She looks stunning in a red, over the top, full-length dress that touches the floor. Her hair is slicked back and when her eyes meet mine, her red lips stretch across her white teeth.

Alcohol clouds her stunning brown eyes. The V at the front of her dress stops at her belly button, showing off her tanned, toned stomach. She walks towards me with all she's worth. If I was any other man, I would see how fucking dangerous Maria is right now.

She takes a glass of champagne off the bar without taking her eyes off me. It's hard not to look away from her, she's stunning.

"What's this for?" I ask as I take the champagne from her.

"To my husband." She clinks her glass with mine and takes a sip.

I'm not amused by her at all. "You're pissed at me?"

She throws her head back and laughs, drawing the attention of everyone in the room.

I smile at them all before I stare at Maria. "You have my attention." I tell her through gritted teeth. That's obviously what she wants.

She stops. "I don't get mad. I get even." She leans in and places a kiss on my cheek before walking away.

Gripping her arm, I smile at her and drag her back to me. "Whatever you're planning, call it off now."

Her smile leaves her face. "Or what?"

I flash her a warning look that I know she won't listen to. A couple passes us.

"He can't keep his hands off me." She tells them while laughing.

I'm not laughing. This isn't fucking funny.

She pulls her arm from me. "Enjoy your party." She's already had too much to drink; I can see it in the sway of her hips. The dress leaves nothing to the imagination.

When I look up, I find King looking at me. He doesn't give me his signature grin. He takes a gulp from his brandy glass before turning away.

I seek out Charlie. He's in the kitchen.

"I have no idea," he says before I even ask him what the hell is going on. "She was asking questions about Andrew." Charlie moves in close to me so only I can hear.

"You told her nothing?" I question him. He better not have. I trust Charlie, but the look he's wearing on his face has me questioning him.

"No, but someone else did." He jerks out his chin and I follow where he is looking. Nate is drinking a beer while flirting with a blonde.

I march over to him and grab him by the back of his neck. "A word." I grip him as I move him through the hallway and out the front door. No one questions me and I draw a few odd looks.

"What did you tell Maria?" I ask the moment I release him. I close the door behind me.

He glares at me as he rubs his neck. "I'm fucking sorry. She tricked me." I can believe that.

"You only think with your dick." He's a moron.

He stops rubbing his neck. "Can you blame me?"

I clear the space between us and my fist collides with his smart mouth. He reels back. "That's my wife you're talking about," I remind him.

His hand covers his mouth before coming away with blood. He spits a mouthful of red liquid out onto my driveway.

"Sorry."

His apology won't save him. "What did you tell her?"

"That he was stabbed." Nate's standing now, ready for the next blow.

"Are you brain dead?" I fire out, when he opens his mouth to answer, I hold up my hand and he spits another mouthful of blood onto my driveway.

"Clean that up and then get the fuck off my property. Don't ever let me see you again."

His mouth hangs open. "Ah, Damien, I fucked up. But don't kick me out."

I'm back in his face. "The next time I see you, you'll be joining Andrew."

I walk away and back into the house. I flex my fist as I search for my wife who's laughing again. She's had far too much to drink.

"You need to control her better." King's words have me flexing my hand again.

"Says you?" If he's trying to make an enemy out of me he's going about it the right way.

"Yes. Says me." His eyes twinkle from drugs, and a drugged up King is a dangerous one.

"She's my wife." I remind him before I walk away and grit my teeth. This charade is ending now as I march over to Maria. I don't know what she sees in my eyes, but she reaches for something to her left before raising her glass and tapping a silver knife along the side of it. The music stops and she looks at me before smiling at the crowd. She has everyone's attention. She'd already had it.

"Thank you all for coming here tonight." They all cheer and I'm ready to end this, before this goes any further.

"Maria." I call her. There is a moment of hesitation in her eyes. I have no idea what she has planned, but I'm pleading with her to stop this.

She glances back at the crowd. "This party is for my husband Damien. I have something very important to tell him."

My stomach twists when she looks at me. She's wearing her scorn so fucking clearly now. It's not hidden behind her smile or batting eyelashes. No, it's on full display for the world to see.

"I want a divorce."

CHAPTER SEVENTEEN

MARIA

I swear he pales at my words. "I want a divorce." I repeat and he's moving. No one around me speaks. I do hear a few people clear their throats, but I don't take my eyes off Damien as he reaches me. Champagne sloshes across my hand as he grabs me and pulls me out of the room. I'm ready to protest as I try to yank my arm from his iron hold, with no success. This wasn't the reaction I was expecting. I'm not exactly sure what I thought was going to happen, but it wasn't this level of anger.

"Get everyone out." Damien speaks to Charlie who doesn't look at me, but moves into the sitting room we had just vacated.

"Party's over." Charlie's deep voice has everyone moving. A few grumbles, and I don't care. I don't know these people. I still have a bit of champagne in my glass and I finish it as the house starts to empty out in record time. I suppose my announcement killed the atmosphere.

I try to pull my hand out of Damien's again, he's crushing my fingers but he won't let me go. I think of screaming at the top of my lungs, but King is in front of us. He will have Damien releasing me in a second. I keep my smile at bay.

"What are you doing?" His snarl surprises me. "Are you fucking stupid?" I flinch at his angry words towards me. I don't get to respond as King disappears. Damien steps in front of me and I finally get my hand back. I'm stunned at King's anger.

"Get out of my home."

My heart pounds. I've never heard Damien so calm, it's deadly.

King laughs and I'm ready to intervene.

"Don't forget who you're talking to." I hear the threat in King's words. My palms grow sweaty. I don't want these two to go up against each other.

Damien takes a step towards King, he's taller and wider but my brother is still formidable. I glance around and see Charlie and Jack standing close to the stairs, watching. The house is nearly empty, glasses and food sit on every available space.

"Kane's son, that's who I'm talking to."

King nods. "Exactly." His eyes dance with anger.

"Don't forget who I am." Damien's words hold a menace I've never heard before. Fear starts to take root and blossoms through my stomach.

"I already told you to control her." I'm stepping out from behind Damien. What the hell?

"King..." I start, stunned at my brother's words. His eyes cut to me and I swallow.

"She's not your problem." Damien sidesteps, blocking me again from King's view.

"She's my sister, so she's my problem."

Damien moves and a startled scream leaves my lips, as he grabs King and pins him against the wall.

"She's my wife, now leave my home."

My stomach quivers as King stares up at Damien with a promise in his eyes. Damien releases him and I'm holding my breath. King fixes his suit jacket and doesn't look at me, as he pulls the front door open. "You're a dead man." He smiles at Damien and closes the door without looking at me.

"Charlie, make sure that clown leaves my property." Damien turns away from the door and the full force of his stare lands on me.

Charlie and Jack slip out the front door and I try to bury my fear as Damien grabs my arm again and starts up the stairs.

"What are you doing?" I try to pull away and he stops on the third step. His eyes bore into me but he doesn't say anything before he continues up the stairs. I glance back at the empty hallway and wonder what I have gotten myself into. My eyes snap to the belt around his waist and fear along with an excitement rope together in my stomach. We clear the last step and Damien doesn't let me go. We pass my room and his. He opens the double doors to the master bedroom that's never been used. He pushes me in and only then does he release me. I glare at him as I rub my hand.

Damien flicks on the light. "Get ready for bed." It's a growl and my core tightens with excitement. His large frame fills the window as he draws the curtains closed. When he turns to me, I still haven't moved.

I fold my arms across my chest. I have no clue what he wants. Does he think he can put me to bed and leave again and that's it? This all disappears? He pulls off his tie roughly. The anger has him clicking his fingers at me.

"Take off your clothes."

A part of me bristles at his tone but I reach back and pull down the zip of my dress. I've only a pair of panties on underneath. The dress has a built in bra. I let the red material pool at my feet. Damien's eyes darken as he angrily opens buttons on his shirt. My breasts grow heavy when he pulls the shirt off. His wide shoulders and muscular chest looks bigger than I remember. I step out of the dress and kick off the shoes.

My excitement grows when he touches the belt of his trousers. The thought of a repeat of last night has me biting my lip. My heart is pumping harder. He drops his trousers and removes his shoes. Damien approaches me when he's in nothing but black boxers. Taking my hand gentler this time, he leads me to the master bed. I'm confused as he pulls back the blankets and tells me to get in. I climb in with lots of hesitation. What's going on?

My confusion grows when Damien walks around to the other side of the bed and gets in. My stomach twists. He pummels his pillows before turning over. His scarred back becomes my focus and I want to trace each mark that was left on his perfect body. The room plunges into darkness.

"What's happening?" I ask the dark room. I had just asked for a divorce and now I'm in the marital bed.

"This is what you wanted." His words are growled and I close my eyes as the room is flooded with light.

"This is what you caused a scene over. Because we didn't share a bed."

I'm ready to deny it, but it's true. I glare at Damien and he's waiting for me to deny it.

"You got what you wanted. Now go to sleep." His bark ends as the room is plummeted into darkness.

I lie down and some part of me smiles. "You don't have to stay so far away from me." I tell the darkness.

He exhales heavily and shifts.

"I mean there is no point sharing a bed with a corpse."

He moves again.

I glance in his direction. "I'd like it if you spooned me." I don't know why I had to be so direct with him all the time.

A scream leaves my lips as he drags me across the bed and my back hits his chest.

"Are you happy now?" His growl fills my ear.

I smile. "Yes." I can't stop the smile as I nestle into his warm body. His erection pushes up against my ass and I'm tempted to wiggle against it to see what he does.

"You're a psycho," he whispers, and I'm not offended because behind his anger I can hear his amusement.

I shift and his arms tighten around me. "Stop it, Maria."

"I just moved." I try and sound innocent. His anger is turning me on. I know I should be afraid with all that just happened, but right now, being in Damien's arms, makes it all worth it. I try and turn but his grip is too tight.

"I can't sleep like this. Loosen your hold." He does and I turn so I'm facing him. I move close enough for my breasts to brush up against his chest. His breath quickens across my forehead.

I feel such a sense of victory. "That's better." I smile and snake an arm around his waist. My fingers move across his back and he stiffens.

"What do you want, Maria?" His voice is low and controlled.

"You." My heart beats a little faster.

"I don't think we can get much closer."

He grows still again beside me. My fingers move of their own accord across his back.

"Tell me what happened to your back?" I'd asked once before and he had shot me down.

"Can you please just go to sleep?" He sounds exhausted and a part of me is ready to let this lie.

"No." I need to know everything about him and if it takes me threatening him with divorce, then that's what I will do.

"I have the divorce papers downstairs." I remind him. The warmth leaves and a cold breeze fills the space. The room is flooded with light and he's over me. My hands are pinned over my head and my stomach plummets. I've gone too far.

His jaw is clenched as he straddles me, leaning in close to my face.

"I'm going to educate you now. So you better listen."

I nod my head as my chest rises and falls quickly. He's scaring me and I don't like it.

"This marriage won't end. There is no divorce or way out." His eyes roam across my face and I see a possessiveness I haven't seen before.

His hands lean heavier on mine, painfully. "Do you understand?" I nod as I fight the onslaught of tears that burn my eyes.

I can't breathe as his lips slam down on mine. I have no idea what is happening. His hands leave mine and roam across my body, sending a wave of tingles rushing through my system. His large erection pushes against my stomach and my panties grow damp instantly. Damien leaves me and I'm breathless and wanting more.

"Turn over." His command is said while he runs his hands through his hair.

I turn on my stomach and the weight of him is heavy on my back. It's crushing but it leaves quickly. Pain burns along my hips as he tears the panties from me. I try to look at him over my shoulder but he pushes my head down into the pillow. Fear curls in my stomach.

"Don't move." His words are accompanied by his fingers entering me. I tighten my hold on the pillow as he plunges two fingers into me, I groan and arch my back, trying to give him more access to me. His fingers sink deeper into me and I'm pushing myself down on them. My release tonight is so close. Damien removes his fingers and I glance at him as he kneels up. He's breathing heavy. I turn around and lie on my back while spreading a leg either side of him.

I want him.

He's struggling with some internal war, but finally he moves closer. His fingers fill me again and I grip his shoulders, pulling him to me. It doesn't take much for me to reach the peak again. Pleasure bubbles through my body as Damien watches me. I groan loudly as a third finger enters me.

"Oh, Damien," I cry out, so close to coming. Something primal fills his eyes at his name, and he rolls his thumb across my clit.

"Come for me," his command is growled and my body obeys, releasing itself across his fingers. I cry out at the ecstasy as my body pulses and throbs. After coming down, Damien slowly removes his fingers. His erection seems larger now and I'm waiting for him to remove his boxers.

He's staring down at me like he doesn't know what to do.

"You're not kicking me out," I say just in case that thought has crossed his mind.

My words snap him out of his turmoil and he moves back over to his side of the bed. The room is plunged into darkness. I yelp as I'm dragged across to his side where he wraps me in his arms.

"Good night, Maria." His growl is odd, after he places a kiss on my forehead.

I open my mouth.

"Don't." He warns.

I close it. "I was..."

"Please."

I exhale loudly. "Fine. Goodnight, Damien."

CHAPTER EIGHTEEN

MARIA

I've been awake for a while now. I've managed to get out of the bed, get dressed into a nightdress, brush my teeth and climb back in. Damien's still asleep on his belly. The quilt rests just at his waistline and I can't take my eyes off his damaged back. My stomach twists. The pain must have been unimaginable. My hand hovers over the wounds and I tighten my fists, not wanting to stir him. My gaze flickers up to his face. He looks peaceful. A smile pulls at my lips but leaves as I refocus my attention on his back. How young was he when this happened? My stomach tightens when I picture a younger version of Damien in pain.

"You're fascinated with ugly things?"

His harsh voice startles me and my heart pounds. "It's not ugly." I frown at the scars. I would never call them ugly. It's a painful story painted on his back. I want to know what happened.

"It's pain." I manage to say. I flicker my gaze at Damien again. If he hadn't spoken I would think he was still asleep. How long has he been awake?

His lids open and his dark green eyes pin me to the spot. "They don't hurt."

I nod. "But the memory would hurt," I say, waiting for him to shut down.

"Yes."

I don't move a muscle as Damien grips the pillow and makes it smaller under his head. His chin now rests on it so he isn't looking at me fully.

"I was fourteen."

A crack appears in my heart as I gaze at his side profile.

"I had stolen a peach."

"A peach?" I didn't want to interrupt him. But he couldn't have been beaten so badly for a God damn peach. A tide of anger rises in me.

"I was raised with the brothers of Melefont. My mother gave me up and they had a zero tolerance policy. So, yes I was beaten over a peach."

He turns over, cutting off the view of his back. His mother gave him up. My mind keeps looping back to that one line. I want to reach for him, but his eyes warn me against it. I kneel up on the bed. "Was the peach nice?"

"I wouldn't know." I had expected my question to make him smile, but instead his eyes grow darker and more distant. "It wasn't for me."

I tighten my hands together waiting for him to tell me who it was for, but he climbs out of the bed.

"Was it for a girl?" The thoughts of him stealing for a girl had jealousy burning my abdomen.

Damien pulls open the curtains, letting light into the room.

"It was for my brother."

Damien doesn't turn back around and for the first time I'm glad he doesn't face me. I can hear it in how his voice cracks, I can see it in the tightness of his shoulders. I can see it in every scar. My chest tightens like a vise has been placed around it. I know it, like I know it's air that I'm pulling into my lungs.

He's dead.

His brother is dead.

I have so many things I want to ask. Who did it? How did it happen? What age was he? Did you track the person down? I want to hurt them so badly.

"He tried to stop them from hurting me."

More silence, that's filling up with so much pain, so much torture. My eyes burn and the vision of Damien wavers in front of me.

"They killed him for it."

A tear makes a pathway down my face and the salty liquid enters my mouth.

"They killed him and I could only watch."

I hold it all in and wipe the tear away as he exhales loudly. He turns to me hesitantly and slowly. My lip trembles and I bite it to stop the onslaught of emotions that pound in my blood, heating it up, making it boil with anger, with pain and with a want for vengeance. "Did you get the person who was responsible?"

His smile is savage. "Yes. Every last one of them."

Fear skitters across my skin, but I clamp down on it. I want details, yet I don't.

"Your mother?" I ask instead and his smile dissolves.

"She's dead."

My abdominal quivers and I pull my knees up to my chin. "Did you kill her?"

Damien's laughter surprises me but also puts my tightened structure at ease.

"No, I never hated her. She was an addict and couldn't mind us. That wasn't her fault." His compassion is real and once again, I'm surprised by him.

"What about your parents"? He asks me and I'm ready to shrug but he just shared a huge chunk of his past with me.

"As you know, my dad is very protective. My mother is not very motherly," I say, trying to find the words. It's something I never talk about. I don't think it really affects me in life. She just never has time for me. It feels odd to think she doesn't like me, but that's how it feels sometimes.

Damien makes his way back to the bed, his heavy green eyes are focused on me and I feel the power of him. Some part of me feels ten feet tall to have his full and undivided attention.

"She favors King and that's okay." I say quickly. "Mothers and their sons." Shit, that sound horrible after what he told me.

"I'm sorry."

Damien shakes his head. "Don't be. You're right. Mothers do seem to lean more towards their sons. But, you said she isn't motherly. You mean motherly to you?"

I tighten my hold on my knees. "I suppose." I hadn't really thought of it like that. Like she could be motherly with King, but not me. I shrug and release my knees. "She never hurt me," I speak to my knees. "She just ..." I don't know.

"Ignored you." Damien finishes and my head snaps up to his. My heart pumps a little harder. "Yeah, I suppose so." I don't want to talk about me anymore.

"Do you always remember her the same?" Damien's interest is intense and I want to keep it on me.

"No." I answer honestly. In the safety of this moment, I tell him. "I know you mean as in, did she ever show me affection, but I sometimes remember her looking differently." My face heats up, it sounds silly. I know. "I always picture her reading to me, but she had green eyes and brown hair, her face was softer." My body buzzes and I hate the feeling of uncertainty I get.

I can't look at Damien. It's something that bothers me. I must have had a fascination with some mother from a program. I've spent far too many hours looking over story books, programs to try to see where this woman came from. I could never find her. All I have is a blonde-haired woman with brown eyes who looks at me with such an absence. Father said I have her eyes. I don't see it, but I never correct him.

Damien hasn't spoken and I realize I've been stuck in my head for too long. "My mother has blonde hair and brown eyes." I point at my own eyes. "That's where I get these from." I exhaled loudly, knowing I wasn't making sense to him.

"What age were you when the brown haired woman read to you." My face heats up further. He must think I'm crazy. He told me last night I'm a psycho. Maybe I am.

"It must have been from a film and I just wanted that kind of mother." I laugh, but it sounds strained. Damien doesn't speak. "Maybe I was three or four. Can you have memories that young?" I frown, hating the feeling that's crawling across my skin.

Damien smiles and it lifts everything in the room. "I wonder, were you as much trouble then as you are now?"

"Me, trouble?" I point at myself as Damien moves closer to me.

"I have never met anyone who has caused me so much trouble. So you as a child must have been something."

"You think that's why my mother treats me so badly?"

His grin slips and his eyes widen.

I grin. "I'm joking. Bad joke." It was easier to reach for.

"I have a meeting this morning, but when I get back, I have a surprise for you."

His wicked grin has my eyes trailing across his wide chest. "What kind of surprise?"

He climbs off the bed and I notice his growing erection.

"You will have to wait."

I keep waiting for the backlash of what I did last night. "What are you going to do about King?"

Damien's eyes darken considerably as he tugs on trousers. "Don't worry about him."

"I can talk to him." I will. The way he spoke to me last night was uncalled for. It was out of character for him, but I refuse to let it go.

"No. I will have a word. Everything will be fine." Damien drags a shirt across his chest and I feel disappointed as I see all that skin disappear.

"What am I meant to do?" I don't want him to go, but I don't want to sound needy either.

"Charlie will be here soon and you can help him clean up the mess downstairs."

I lie back on the bed, covering my face with my hands. I speak through my fingers. "I don't know what is worse, cleaning or Charlie."

The bed dips and Damien pulls my hands away. His brows are drawn down. "Did Charlie do something?" He's holding my hands either side of my head and I love the position we are in.

"What? No." Now I want to say yes. I love the angry look in his eyes. "Maybe," I say slowly and wiggly my body closer to him. His eyes burn across my chest and his gaze slowly drags up to my eyes.

Damien's eyes narrow. "Maria, tell me."

I bite my lip. "He's so serious. I can't make him laugh."

Relief swims in Damien's eyes. "He likes jokes." Damien's eyes are a light green as he smiles. It's a secret smile.

"I don't have any jokes." I'm not a comedian.

Damien puts on a tie. "A man walks into a shoe shop. He says: Give me a pair of shoes, please." Damien shifts his voice and continues. "Certainly, sir, what size?" Another shift in his voice, "I wear a twelve but I'll take a six." He answers himself, "why, sir? Are they for someone else?"

I love how Damien is alternating his voice. That alone is funny and I suppress a laugh until I hear the punch line.

"Oh, they're for me. They'll be too tight, but when I take them off, it'll be the one moment of pleasure I experience all day."

Damien pulls on his shoes. "That's not very funny." I say.

He grins. "I saw you smile. Trust me. Charlie will love it."

I feel like I'm being set up. Surprise flitters through me as Damien leans in and places a kiss on my lips, it's soft at first but hardens. "I want to fuck you."

His words have my body coming alive. "Then do." I offer as I push my lips harder against his.

He groans and pulls away. "I will, just not now." The promise I hang onto as he leaves the room.

CHAPTER NINETEEN

DAMIEN

I hate leaving her, especially when she sounded so vulnerable earlier speaking about her mother. I hate deceiving her; it seems wrong, but there's more at stake and I need all the facts.

Charlie has turned up trumps with research into the O'Brien's. He found a family who had reported their daughter missing twenty-two years ago. She was three when she went missing. The case is still open; they've never stopped searching for her and I have an appointment with Mary O'Brien.

Charlie enters the house and I try not to look around me at the mess from last night.

"I'll be gone a while today. If King comes around, ring me," I say. I don't want him near her until I figure out his end game.

"No problem." Charlie carries a paper under his arm as he walks into the kitchen. I follow him and when he notices me behind him he raises a brow.

"She's going to tell you a joke this morning. You have to laugh."

He frowns. "I don't laugh."

"I know. But I'm paying you to laugh at her joke."

Charlie nods and I feel satisfied as I leave.

It takes two hours before I arrive at the O'Brien's residence. My phone rings as I get out of the car after being allowed in on the property.

"Hello." I answer the unknown number.

"Mr. Callan, your Chihuahua is ready for collection." I push up my sleeve and check the time. "I'll collect it around three." I say.

"Perfect, see you then."

Pushing my phone into my pocket, I face the house. It's large enough to look like a miniature hotel. The ivy that grows along the bottom floor is green and red, the way it twines together is done in perfect sync. A lot of time must have gone into the precision of the way it was planted. I like it.

The white front door opens and my heart does a little skip when I meet Mary's smiling green eyes. Dark hair is pulled back and I'm trying to picture her reading to Maria.

"Mrs. O'Brien. Thank you for seeing me." I offer my hand and she accepts it before moving back.

"Please, come in, Robert."

"Thank you." I step into a white hallway that's polished and museum like. I imagine if I raise my voice it would echo through the stunning space that lets light in. I look up and see the window several stories above us. A tunnel has been cut out allowing the light to pour perfectly into the hall.

"Stunning," I say to Mary.

She smiles softly at me. "It's my husband's design, but yes, I do agree." She closes the door and I follow her into what I would expect from a house of this grandeur. It's decorated with golds and mint greens. The color pallet makes me want to relax.

"I know you said you're new to the staff, but I've answered these questions so many times."

I sit down on an armchair and remove a notepad and pen from my pocket. Giving Mary a soft smile, I try to put her at ease. "The case was handed to me and I know you have answered everything, but I just want to make sure we aren't missing anything."

She nods, but her lips tighten into a thin line. "The staff turnover isn't a great sign. I only had Andrew here a few weeks back."

Andrew? He was very stupid for using his real name. So he had met her. "I know. But I'm on the case now and I have a very high record of solving cases.

I hate the sadness that enters her eyes. "You're very young but we've been searching for twenty-two years." She swallows and looks away. "It's funny that you arrived today." When she looks back at me, her eyes swim with pain that I don't understand. Pain I don't want to understand.

"She would be twenty-five today." Would be. She thinks she's dead. Maria's birthday is today and she's stuck with Charlie. Why didn't she tell me?

"Tell me about the day she went missing."

She frowns before all emotions get buried and she tells a story of a little girl looking at monkeys in the zoo. "Maria loved the zoo."

Some part of me caves. They never changed her name.

"So we took her weekly. Anyway, one minute she was there and the next she was gone. We had them close the zoo down, but she was never found."

Mary looks away from me. "Do you have enemies? Was there ever a ransom?" They are extremely wealthy, but I know there wasn't a ransom. I want to know why Kane took her.

"No ransom. No phone calls. Nothing. She vanished that day and that is it. It was like she never existed."

Her pain peeks out at me.

I scribble in the notepad. "Any enemies?"

She looks away from me again. "Honestly, I blame my husband."

I close the notepad. "Why is that?"

"I've told this to Carl."

Carl, who the fuck is Carl?

"With so many of you coming over the last few weeks, it's really made each day more difficult." Guilt swells in her eyes at feeling angry that we are making her remember Maria. Jesus, my Maria.

"I promise I'm the last. I do apologize and can only imagine how difficult this must be."

I open my notepad and let my pen hover over it. She moves in the armchair across from me before she speaks.

"It seems quite daft now, but at first it was something I was convinced of, because of the timing."

I nod. But I just want her to tell me.

"My husband made a deal over cigars and brandy with a close associate. That when they had children, they would marry each other." She laughs at the stupidity of what she is saying. "The relationship turned sour and they grew distant." She shrugs.

"So you think this associate has something to do with Maria's disappearance?"

She tightens her hands together. "If my husband knew I was telling you about this, he wouldn't be happy." She smiles at me. "It's a good job. I don't care what he thinks."

I smile now and something in me hurts. I see Maria. I see Maria in this woman. Her mother.

The defiance. The fight, and even in her face, I can see snippets of Maria.

Kane, you evil bastard.

"When Maria disappeared, so did his associate. The cops couldn't find him and that's when I turned to your firm to investigate it privately, but nothing was ever found."

To think Maria has been so close to her real parents and all this wealth couldn't find her. It showed me the lengths that Kane went to hide her. Was it over a sour deal? Deals made in the underworld are normally written in blood. It isn't something you can back out of. But to take a child. Did he take her for King? My stomach twists painfully.

Who is taking the photos? Has Mary hired someone new? But that would mean she knows about Maria. Which I don't believe she does.

She rises now and I see her age in how her shoulders hang. "That is all I have for you."

I pocket the notepad. "Just one more question. Can I speak to your husband?"

"If you can, let him know I'm looking for him too."

"Your husband is missing?"

She waves it off. "He does this sometimes. Especially around her birthday. I'm sure he will return in a few days."

I nod and thank Mary for helping me.

"There's something in your file that made me smile." I pause at the door. "You read to Maria each night."

Mary's green eyes fill with suspicion. "I don't recall telling anyone that." She frowns.

"It was earlier on in the investigation. You must have been traumatized when you mentioned it. Sorry for bringing it up."

"No, it's fine. Ask your question, Robert."

"I have a daughter, she loves to read, so I was wondering about the bedtime stories. Were there any in particular you would recommend?"

Her smile is pure and her pain is raw. "Dick and Jane. Maria loved Dick and Jane." Her eyes water and she reaches out and squeezes my arm.

"You keep your little girl safe."

I nod at her. Feeling like a bastard.

She releases me. "Can you tell the other investigators that I'm tired and I think it's time I close the case." She holds her head high like it might push the pain away.

"Of course. We have two Carl's, I'm not sure which one is on this case."

"The handsome one." She laughs, but it doesn't reach her eyes. "The one with the scar," she says now as she holds the door.

"Ah, Carl with the scar on his lip," I say.

She nods. "Yes, thank you, Robert."

King has been here. He has been here with Maria's mother and he knows who she is. He must have found out that Andrew had been here too. That's why Andrew's dead.

King must have killed him. That night at the house, he had dismissed Andrew's death and taken us to the charity ball. He wanted it to be forgotten.

"Thank you once again, Mary." I take her hand and place a kiss on it. Her green eyes widen in surprise. I wish I could tell her.

I release her hand and she steps in and closes the door.

My mind won't slow down as I think of everything I've learned. So Kane must have taken Maria once Maria's father didn't keep to the deal. Why did Maria's father not beg for Maria and agree to the marriage? What is so deep-rooted that Maria was never returned? What are Kane's plans for her now? Will she finally be given to King? Is that why I'm not allowed to touch her?

My foot slams down on the peddle of the car. He is one sick fucker. What makes this all worse is Kane's wife. She must know since she's ignored Maria her whole life. My heart pounds in my chest and I want to hurt someone, kill someone.

I want to kill King and Kane for what they have done to Maria.

We have so much in common. We were both robbed of a childhood. I have scars on my flesh, but when Maria finds out who she is, the scars will cut deep inside her. I just need to find a way to ease that pain as much as possible. Her demanding attitude makes more sense to me. She's craving attention, craving to belong to someone or something. She must have always felt such a disconnect from them. I know Kane is an evil bastard, but this turns my stomach—and as for that cunt King, they'll both pay.

CHAPTER TWENTY

MARIA

Charlie laughed at my joke. Like it was a knee slapper. It scared me a little with how hard he laughed and when he was done, he started to read the paper again. The whole thing makes me uncomfortable. The phone has been buzzing all morning. It's King. I ignore him. I will talk to him, but he needs to stew for a little while longer. I'm not going to just forgive him that easily for talking to me the way he did.

I shower and get dressed into black jeans and a red shirt. It's simple, but I take my time with my appearance. I place my hair in pigtails and then decide I look silly. Pulling them out, I return downstairs as the front door opens. I'm excited, but it dwindles quickly.

"Hello, sweetheart."

I clear the last three steps and walk into my father's outstretched arms.

"Hi, daddy."

I know he's here to start about what I did with Damien. "Before you say anything, I wasn't really going to do it," I tell him.

My father watches me carefully and I get an uneasy feeling. I keep still until it passes.

"When will you learn?" He takes my face in both his hands, his touch is gentle but his words are sharp. "So defiant."

"I get that from you," I grin at him and he smiles, releasing my face.

"I'm sorry." I apologize because I hate disappointing him.

"If Damien forgives, so will I. Where is he?" I start to walk into the kitchen where Charlie was. He was reading his paper, but he's not here now.

"He's away at a meeting. He should be back soon. He's been gone ages."

"He left you alone?" My father steps into the Kitchen and I put on the kettle.

"No. Charlie is here."

I turn and smile at my father.

"Has Damien forgiven you?" My father asks while sitting down. He's an older version of King; it's uncanny how much they look alike.

"Yes, but I haven't forgiven King." I fold my arms across my chest.

"What happened?" Father frowns.

"He was rude to me last night." I don't want to say the F word in front of my father.

"He's protective. That's his job."

"I'm not a job, daddy," I say as I get two cups down.

I hate the protective shit. It drives me mad. I try to reel in my frustration.

"You are to King. Don't be too hard on him. He loves you."

I pour out our teas and bring them to the table. "I love him too, but that doesn't mean I'll make it easy."

My father's laughter is quick and warms me. "I'm sure you won't. You never have."

I sip the tea.

The front door opens and I'm up and out of my seat. I take two steps into the hall and my heart swells.

"What is that?"

Damien's smile is instant. "Happy Birthday." He holds out a white fluffy Chihuahua that wriggles in his huge arms.

"Is this my surprise?" I ask and his smile widens as he holds out the dog to me.

"One of them."

I take it and I have no idea why he would get me a dog. I'm not exactly an animal lover. But he looks so proud watching me. "Thank you. But it's not my birthday." The dog tries to lick my face and I'm ready to put it down. I'm tempted to ask him if he kept the receipt.

"Damien." My father has stepped into the hall and the atmosphere in the space changes.

"Kane, I didn't see your car." Damien places two shopping bags down on the floor. I want to see what's in them, but I watch Damien.

"I walked, I was in the area." That's odd, father walking.

The dog yips in my arms and I nearly let it fall. It better not pee on me.

"What made you think it was Maria's birthday?" My father reaches for the dog and I quickly give him it.

"I thought she had mentioned something about her birthday."

There is a desperation clinging to Damien and it's so odd to see it in his eyes.

"Oh, what I said this morning."

He nods.

"Yeah, I just wanted presents," I say and shrug.

My father smiles at me. "Is this the birthday present?" He asks Damien.

I'm giving my father a look that he doesn't heed.

"She doesn't like animals."

I laugh. "No. That's when I was younger." I try to lighten the mood.

"Like a toddler?" Damien asks.

My childhood hadn't left my mind this morning and it obviously hadn't left Damien's, either.

I look to my dad. "What age was I?"

I can't think.

"From the start of time, you've disliked animals." My father hands me back the dog and I'm tempted not to take it. "It's cute."

My father laughs, but something is off.

I glance at Damien; he's tense as he stares at my father.

"Damien." I take a step towards him and he looks at me. "Did your meeting go okay?" God, maybe something went wrong.

He forces a smile. "Yeah, it went perfect."

"Was it work related?" My father asks and I take the dog into the kitchen.

"Yes. For my security company." I hear Damien say.

The dog yips and I drop it to the floor. It might be thirsty. I grab a bowl and fill it with cold water. Turning around it's gone. When I step back into the hall it's in Damien's arms. I smile. It looks cute in his arms.

"I was trying to talk to you about King," Damien says.

My father glances at me before turning back to Damien. "I'll have a word with him."

"He threatened my life." Dear God, Damien is so serious. I want to tell him to calm down. King was just worked up.

"He's very protective of his sister and you told him she wasn't his problem anymore."

"Daddy." I'm staring at my father with wide eyes. "That doesn't give him the right to threaten my husband." King has shown quite the temper lately and it isn't fair to Damien to be caught up in the firing line.

"Your husband." My father looks at me differently.

"Yeah." I feel like I need to say it slowly. Why was everyone acting so weird?

"I'll have a word with King." My father addresses Damien. "You can come over tonight for drinks."

"Am I not invited?" I ask my father.

"It's just the boys, maybe spend some time with your mother." I cringe. Since I moved out I haven't seen her, she doesn't ring me either.

"Yeah, I'll see." I place a kiss on his cheek. Damien stares at him as he leaves the house and the hostility in Damien's eyes has me waiting until my father leaves.

"You want to tell me what's going on?"

He shakes his head. "Nothing. Why?"

My hand automatically goes to my hip. "I lied about my birthday. Why?"

Damien moves towards me. The stupid dog wriggles closer to his chest. "I don't know Maria. I mean, you are the one who lied."

I exhale a short laugh. "Are you serious? You looked like a drowning man. I just threw you a rope."

His eyes harden. "I don't know what you are talking about. You asked for a dog in Rome, so I assumed it was your birthday."

I grin at Damien, but I'm pissed. "You're such a liar."

He pushes the dog into my hands and heads up stairs. I have no idea what is happening.

Charlie comes in the back door. "Perfect timing." I tell him and hand him the dog.

He holds up both his hands. "Is that a rat?"

"It's a dog." I push it towards him again and he takes a step back.

"I don't like it."

"It's tiny." I shove it towards him again. "Take it." I force some authority into my voice and he does. I give Charlie's arm a pat. "Thank you."

Turning, I march upstairs to see what is wrong with my husband.

"What's going on? Why are you acting so weird?" I say and try not to get distracted as Damien pulls off his shirt.

"I don't know what you are talking about, Maria."

"Don't make me sound crazy." My temper flares.

"Then don't act crazy." He shouts back and I jump, startled by his outburst. He glares at me and it's like all the life is sucked out of him. Sitting on the bed, he places his head in his hands.

"What's happening?" Fear clutches my chest and I go to my knees. I need to see his face. "Damien," I say his name softly. "Is it what we talked about this morning. About your brother." My heart bounces around in my chest.

"No." His eyes clear and he takes my face in his hands. They are so large and consume me. "You're so beautiful."

The way he says it has me swallowing. "Thank you."

"What's going on?" I cover his hands with mine.

"It's work," he says, and this time it's more convincing, but I don't think it's all the truth. I don't push him.

"Are you going to fuck me now?"

His eyebrows rise in surprise and his lips tug up. "You're so naughty using bad words."

I laugh. "I almost should be punished."

"Is that what you want Maria? You want me to punish you?" His tone changes and everything in me is more aware, more alert.

"Do whatever you want." I press my lips against his and he doesn't respond. My hand trails along his trousers and I palm his huge erection. He breathes into my face and I feel powerful at his reaction.

My hand runs along his cock again and I'm transported back to the shower in Rome.

"Take it out," I tell him before planting another kiss on his lips.

"I thought I got to do whatever I wanted."

I look into Damien's eyes. "I changed my mind."

His grin is wicked. "That sounds like you." He stands and opens his belt. I don't move off the floor as he pushes his trousers and boxers down. His erection springs free. I wrap my fingers around it and start to stroke. "Charlie's downstairs." I remind him. His eyes snap to me and something possessive enters them. "I don't share." His words are firm.

"I'm not asking you to." I take the head of his cock into my mouth and suck, he groans but his anger at my statement still lingers.

"Take off your clothes." He takes my arm and brings me up off my knees. I'm ready to object, but the savagery in his eyes, I want. I don't do it slow. I strip down quickly until I'm naked.

"Lie on the bed." I do and instantly spread my legs.

"Touch yourself." I look up at Damien in question as he stands over me stroking his shaft.

I let my hand drift down and touch my clit. I arch up to my hand the moment my fingers hit the bunch of nerves.

"Jesus, you're so hot."

"I want you." I tell him, but I don't stop touching myself. He lets his shaft go and kneels down on the floor so he's in between my thighs. "Put your fingers inside. I want to watch you." I slip two fingers inside, I'm so wet.

His tongue joins my fingers and I remove mine to give him access. "Oh God." I grip his hair and guide his face deeper. His tongue fills me and I want more. It's not enough.

His tongue leaves me and his fingers immediately fill the space. Kisses are planted on my stomach as Damien makes his way up. He stops at my breasts and I groan as he sucks on my nipple before nipping it with his teeth. His fingers slide out of me and my body is aching and humming for him. His cock rests at my opening as he takes my other breast in his mouth and sucks hard. Too many emotions swirl and I want him so bad. I push my body down, trying to force his cock inside me.

"What do you want?" He asks releasing my breasts.

"You." I tell him as he moves fully up. Without warning, he slams his cock inside me, filling me up quickly. There are no half measures as he plows into me. I groan loudly as he starts fucking me like a man possessed.

CHAPTER TWENTY-ONE

DAMIEN

I'm buried in her and it's not enough. With Maria, it will never be enough. I pull out when I know she's close to coming. I don't want it to end yet. I never want it to end. I stand up and she looks up at me, dazed. "Taste yourself." She crawls to the edge of the bed and takes me in her mouth. I feel the head hit the back of her throat. Fuck me! Her mouth was made for my cock. She's moving faster, her mouth working and I don't want my release to come. I'm so close to spilling my seed in her mouth. I take my cock back and stroke my shaft before moving up to the head of the bed.

"Get on your knees." The wicked glint in her eyes has me wanting to fuck her so hard. She faces the door on all fours. She never closed the double doors and I think it's turning her on. I climb up and settle myself behind her. I'm tempted to fuck her ass, but I'll save that for the next time. Directing my cock, I slide it into her wet, tight pussy. The walls tighten around my cock and I know I won't last long. Being inside Maria has me forgetting everything.

"Fuck me." She's breathing heavy. Her arousal is heavy on my cock. Placing my hand on her lower back, I start to fuck her. Her groans are loud and it has my own release growing fast. I stop and flip her on her back. She's ready to object when I push my cock back into her. My balls hit her ass as I pound myself into her pussy. I can't slow down, I've never pounded so hard but she's perfect around my cock. Her hands pull at her nipples-and fuck me-I can't stop as she groans again and I empty my seed inside her, she cries out her own release and I keep riding her until we are both empty. Both fighting for air.

I land beside her and I take a moment to catch my breath. Glancing at her, she has a smile on her face. "If I smoked, I think I'd have one right now."

"The compliment of the year," I say and stare at the ceiling as my heart pounds too fucking fast in my chest.

The bark of the dog has me looking at Maria. "You abandoned it?"

She grins. "I left it with Charlie." Her cheeks turn red now.

"Charlie, who must have heard us?"

"No." She lies and I face the ceiling again as my heart starts to slow and my mind speeds up. I don't want to think about the fucking mess I'm in. I reach for Maria and pull her into me. Her body rests next to mine and my cock grows hard again. Being buried inside her lets my mind go free. It's more than sex with her. She gives me a place that's filled with peace. Pulling her closer, I look down at her. She's staring up into my face.

"I want a job."

I'm ready to remove her from me. "Not this again," I say instead.

She turns onto her stomach and leans up. "I'm serious. I could work for your security company." Her suggestion is said shyly and I take a moment to look at her. She never got a chance.

"What would you do?"

She chews on her lip. They are still swollen from being around my cock. It twitches now.

"I could be your secretary."

I grin. "I can see that."

She doesn't smile. "Like a real one, Damien. I'm good with people. I could answer the phone and stuff like that."

"Okay," I say.

Her face breaks into a huge smile. "Where is my office?"

"Can't you work from here?"

She sits up and gets off the bed. "No way am I working from home."

I'm regretting my decision already.

She speaks as she pulls on her clothes. "I think we could work from your office."

"My office?" I question getting off the bed.

She pulls up her jeans but stops and walks over to me. Reaching up on the tip of her toes she plants a kiss on my cheek.

"Don't worry about anything. I have it covered."

"We can't share an office." I hate bursting her bubble, but she can't hear the jobs I take.

Her eyes waver.

"But we can give you Terry's."

"Terry the receptionist?" Her hand is on her hip.

"I'll clear out one of the rooms in the hotel as your office."

I walk to her and take her face in my hands. "Okay?" I kiss her softly.

"I suppose. I kind of like the idea of us working together."

"We could meet for lunch once a week," I say.

Her eyes widen, "three times."

I grin. "Fine, three." I put it low because I knew she would fight it.

"No security for me."

I release her face and pull on my boxers. "That's not going to happen."

She quickly puts on her bra. "Damien, I don't understand all the security. I'm not going anywhere."

"You remember those photos you snooped at on the plane."

She nods.

"Someone is watching you." She needs to know the danger.

"Maybe they were watching you." She tells me as she slips on her shirt.

"Does it matter? You are safer with security."

"But I'll be with you." She glances at the door as the dog barks again.

"We'll see," I say.

She smiles in victory and leaves the room. I finish getting dressed and follow her downstairs.

Charlie is still holding the dog. I don't think Maria likes it at all. It cost me fifteen hundred dollars and she didn't give it ten minutes.

"You want the dog?" I ask Charlie.

Maria snaps it out of his hands. "You can't give it away."

"Does it have a name?" I ask Maria as I get myself a coffee from the machine.

"Not yet. But Rome wasn't built in a day." She tucks the dog under her arm.

Charlie won't meet my eye. I slap his arm. "Thanks for the heads up," I say. He knew I was referring to Kane being here.

I leave Maria in the kitchen. "Maybe Rome would be nice," I say over my shoulder and can hear her trying out the name.

"He just arrived on foot."

I'm already nodding as I enter the living room that's been put back together.

"You think he knows?" Charlie asks me.

"I don't know, to be honest." I answer. I'm not sure what Kane knows.

"I just want to say something, but I don't want you to take me the wrong way."

"Charlie, when someone says that, it means they're going to say something that will properly piss me off." I give him the chance to back off.

"She's a business deal," Charlie says and pauses.

"I know." My answer has my stomach curling. I said yes so I could grow my own business. I was her bodyguard. That's all this was ever meant to be. It's what it was.

"Digging into her past is going to get us killed."

I sit down on the couch.

"Rome, come here." Maria's voice carries into the living room.

"I was lied to." I try to defend my actions but I already see it in Charlie's eyes. Does it matter who she is? I'll still get paid the same. I don't like being deceived.

"Is that why you are looking for answers?" Charlie stays standing, and so he should. Charlie runs his hands across his face. "My house was broken into Damien, they destroyed everything."

I sit forward. "You are only telling me this now?" Fuck.

"I can deal with it." Charlie waves me off. Rome races into the room, its tiny nails clicking on the floor. It runs over to my legs and I scoop it up.

"You can stay here. It would make sense; you could watch Maria and you would be safe."

"I can't move in." Charlie starts as Maria enters the room. She's smiling as she looks to Rome.

"I'm not surprised she's in your arms." Her eyes are such a light brown as she walks towards me.

"Charlie is moving in," I say as I pass Rome over to Maria. She takes the dog but the dislike is clear on her face.

"You don't have to keep it."

"Charlie's moving in?" She rubs the dog. "I'm keeping Rome." She adds.

"I don't want to intrude." Charlie starts to apologize.

This is the point where Maria should say, you're not intruding but she continues to rub Rome.

"You're not, Charlie. I insist. So does Maria." I glare at Maria.

She bobs her head. "Can't wait." She leaves the room with Rome.

I don't linger, Charlie has too much to say and I hate how right he is. I'm getting too involved and now I'm wondering when exactly that happened.

Work doesn't help take my mind off Maria.

"Terry, can you get the manifesto for the plane we took to Rome?" I ask him as I gather up all the mail, one of the envelopes is a large A4 yellow one. I open it.

"Yeah, it could take a bit of time."

I glance at Terry. "Try to be quick." I leave with the mail and pull out the photos. It's pictures of Maria again. A smile tugs at my lips. She's walking like a goddess with Nate and Charlie on either side of her. She's a woman on a mission. She's stunning. My eyes move across the image to Nate, who watches her. Charlie is facing away, watching for danger. I flick through the images. It's just her walking through the carpark to the mall. I turn over the images and there is nothing on them. Just someone wants me to know she's being watched. I'm being watched.

I push them back into the envelope and place them in the folder in the desk drawer. Charlie's place being thrashed told me that I'm too close to the truth. King or Kane know I found out Maria's identity. I have a feeling that that's what our drinks will be about tonight.

I try to focus on the contracts I have to finish for my own business. Maria rings three times and each time I tell Terry to take a message. Each time I want to hear her voice. That is dangerous. She's dangerous.

The phone rings again. "I'm sorry, Mr. Callan. She's threatening my job." Terry's voice shakes.

"Put her through."

The line clicks. "Yes, Maria."

"Oh my God. What if something was wrong?"

"Is there something wrong?"

I wait.

She exhales with irritation. "No. But there could have been."

I suppress a smile. "I'm very busy. What is it?"

"Don't make me come down there, Damien." Her threat isn't idle and I sit back in my chair.

"I'm listening."

"I want you home at eight."

"I'm having drinks with your father." I didn't want to, but he was the boss.

"I know, I've spoken to daddy and he knows to have you home by eight." She sounds so smug.

"Well, since you've organized it."

"Good. Because I'm cooking."

I sit forward. Maria didn't strike me as the cooking type. "You're cooking?"

"I'm trying, Damien." There's a vulnerable tone in her voice.

I shouldn't want to comfort her, I shouldn't feel a swell of pride that she's cooking for me.

"I'm sure it will be perfect."

"Good." She sounds nervous. "See you at seven thirty."

"You said eight."

"I changed my mind." The phone goes dead.

I laugh at my empty office. I think I know what she is up to, and then she does the opposite. The idea of divorce papers waiting for me has me gripping the phone. I place it in the receiver and quickly let it go. She won't set me up again.

Will she?

CHAPTER TWENTY-TWO

MARIA

I check the clock again. It's seven forty-five. The table looks so great. The smell from the kitchen makes me proud. I gave Rome to Charlie and set them up in the living room. The idea of Charlie living here clouded all the sexual fantasies I had that starred just me and Damien. But I'll work around it. I could adapt and change. I fix the red napkin on the table so it's parallel with the fork.

My short, green, cocktail dress brushes across my thighs as I move around the kitchen. I open a bottle of wine before stirring the pasta again.

I pour myself a glass and check the time. It's seven fifty. He better get here soon. I take a peek into the living room. Rome has nestled herself against Charlie.

"You got yourself a friend," I say to him. He glances down at Rome but doesn't smile.

"So, just to clarify." I start and take a sip of the wine. "I just put the leg of chicken on top of the pasta and then sprinkle it with that green stuff?"

Charlie sits forward disturbing Rome who gets up, circles, before sitting back down. "Exactly. Just pour a teaspoon of the chicken juices across the chicken before you put the parsley on it."

I'm nodding. "You can't say anything." Charlie had cooked the meal, but I had watched the whole process, so technically I had cooked.

"I won't." Charlie nods seriously. I glance at the small table in front of him that holds some crisps and a coke.

"You need something else before he comes?" I don't want Charlie disturbing us.

"I got everything here, Maria."

The front door opens and butterflies erupt in my stomach. "Okay. Goodnight." I close the door and make my way to the hall. My stomach plummets. Damien looks troubled.

"Everything okay?" I ask and he looks up at me.

Some of the worry disappears, but not enough to make me relax.

"Yeah, just a busy day."

For the first time I feel self-conscious. I made an effort for him. Not to grab his attention, but I wanted to look pretty for him. It was the first time I did something for someone else.

"Food's ready."

He's looking at me and I don't know what to think. He nods and walks towards me. "Let's see what you made."

I move into the kitchen and stir the pasta. "Why don't you sit down."

He does, and when I glance at him, his eyes roam across the table.

"Tell me again why you agreed to this?"

I place the pasta on the plate just like Charlie had said. "Because I just wanted to do something nice for you." Picking up the chicken, I place it on top of the pasta.

"Not the dinner, Maria."

I glance at Damien and stop what I am doing.

"The marriage." His jaw is clenched and the worry still swims in his eyes.

"You want to tell me what happened with my dad?" That's the only explanation for this.

"Just answer me." His brows draw down as he speaks.

"I told you. The money. The freedom."

"Did you always know that your marriage would be arranged?"

I hate that he is bringing this up when I put—Charlie put—so much effort into the meal. I do the little sprinkle thing on the top of the chicken. I think it looks pretty.

"Yes," I answer as I turn to Damien.

My stomach tightens with the look in his eyes. "Did you know who you would marry?"

"I didn't think it would be you. But no, I didn't know exactly who it would be." I place the dinner in front of Damien and he doesn't even look at it.

"What if I'm just temporary?" He says.

My heart pangs. "You can't be." Why would he be? "I married you. I knew it was forever. You said it yourself." He's standing now and I don't know what's going on. I'm looking at the meal I spent hours watching Charlie cook. "Damien."

He shakes his head. "I want you to think. You lived in the same house with Kane."

I want to point out that of course I did, he's my father after all. But the vibes that pulsed from Damien keep my mouth closed. Something is seriously off.

"Who would he have married you off to? He must have mentioned someone. Was there ever anyone around often?"

I try to think. "No." I'm shaking my head. "I mean, security was always around. But, apart from that, I didn't see many people."

"Did he ever mention a family?" Desperation clings to Damien's words and he's frightening me.

"What's happening?"

He won't answer me.

"Sit down and eat the meal I just cooked for you." My voice rises and I start to dish out my own, there isn't much care given as I hate the atmosphere. I sit down and drink half the glass of wine.

"Sit down, Damien." He's still standing.

His phone rings and I dare him to answer it. His eyes clash with mine and he leaves the room.

"Hello."

I drop my knife and fork and try to calm my pounding heart.

I'm tempted to pick up the phone and ask my father what he had said to Damien. Why would he think he was temporary? My father wouldn't make me marry someone else. Not when I gave everything to Damien. This makes no sense. I push my chair out and step into the hall. He's still on the phone and when he notices me he turns.

"Okay, thanks Terry. I appreciate it."

"You want to tell me what is going on?" I fold my arms across my chest.

Damien looks conflicted. "This arrangement we have isn't long term." He doesn't blink.

"I don't understand?" Why does my voice shake?

Damien doesn't even flinch. The hardness in his eyes has discomfort flowing through me. "You've been promised to someone else."

My heart pounds and I'm ready to laugh. I shake my head. "No. I can't be. I married you." I sound dumb, but my father wouldn't do that. "Why are you saying these things?"

"Because they are true."

"How long have you known?"

Damien's eyes shadow with guilt and something in me cracks.

"The contract stated that I couldn't touch you, I assumed that was why?"

I recoil from his words. My stomach shifts and I have to walk away from him. I can't breathe.

"Maria." He's standing behind me and I can't accept what he is saying.

"You touched me." I spin around, my anger turning me inside out. "You took my virginity."

"You weren't complaining." His words are growled.

"Does my father know?" Oh God. My face burns. Did they discuss this? "No."

"You signed a contract." I can't wrap my head around what he is telling me.

"Yes." His eyes don't waver, he holds my gaze firmly like he isn't talking about the precious thing I gave him.

"Do you know who'll be fucking me next?"

A warning flashes in Damien's eyes. "Maria."

"What?" My roar has me wanting to pull the kitchen apart. I hate him.

"Maybe it's Charlie. Let's go ask him." I don't get into the living room before Damien grabs me. My back hits the wall and he boxes me in.

"It's not Charlie."

I refuse to cry. I refuse to show my pain. "Get the fuck off me."

He stands back and lets me go. I want to throw up as I walk back into the kitchen and get my car keys. I return to the hall and he's still standing there.

"Where are you going?"

"To find out who gets me next." Like I'm some kind of disposable thing.

I hear him move before his hand circles my wrist. I'm waiting for it. My hand connects with his face. "Don't touch me."

"This is not my doing!" He grips both my arms. "I didn't ask for this!" He shakes me. "I didn't expect this..." He trails off and his hands tighten on my arms. "I didn't expect you."

"That's all very nice, Damien. But I'm still being passed onto someone else." I pull my arms out of his hands. "I need to find out who."

Damien blocks the door with his large frame. "I can't let you do that."

"Why? If I'm being passed to someone else, I think I have the right to know who." My heart pounds. I want him to tell me he would never let me go. But I already sense that's not how this is going to go.

"Because if he knows we slept together, I'm a dead man."

I'm laughing, my eyes burn. "You're worried about you." I'm nodding my head. "You are such a bastard."

He exhales loudly like I'm being unreasonable. "I just need time."

I want to hurt him so bad. He is dismissing me so easily. He'll pass me on to the next bidder, he just needs time to save his ass first. I don't know why I thought he would want me, why he would fight for me.

No one ever does.

My life motto is there in the forefront of my mind. Don't get mad, get even. But right now, I didn't want revenge. I want someone to tell me they'll fight for me. That I am worth it.

I try to keep the storm that's ripping through me at bay. "I want to speak with my father. I won't mention anything about us."

He doesn't move.

"Move, Damien. Because I'm going to him whether you like it or not."

"I can't let that happen." Damien takes a step towards me and dread curls along the base of my spine.

CHAPTER TWENTY-THREE

DAMIEN

I could walk away a quarter of a million richer—and with my head attached to my shoulders. I entered this agreement for the money—for my business. Kane cut the deal short and let me loose. He said I could have the money, but under one condition. And that one condition is to walk away from Maria. A deal had been made and Maria would be remarried to someone else. He wouldn't say to whom. King had smirked at me, knowing he had won. It made me wonder if she was for him, and now that Terry had told me that King had been on the plane's manifesto to Rome, it identified the photographer. He is the one that had been keeping a close eye on her. Too fucking close—he's sick. I assume he's the one who killed Andrew for finding out who Maria is. So walking away is the wisest thing to do. I can tell that they don't know what Charlie had found out for me. They must have suspected he was looking into Maria, so they roughed up his home. But when I met them they weren't nervous. They don't know the knowledge I have.

If I let her go, she'll get the answer she wants. She might never find out who she really is, but she will find out who she's going to marry next. So why am I stopping her from leaving? I owe her nothing. The fire in her eyes burns too brightly as she stares at me. I also see fear snake its way into her beautiful eyes.

"Wait." I hold up both hands.

Her chest rises and falls in the small cocktail dress. I close my eyes and try to talk myself down off the ledge I'm ready to leap from.

When I open my eyes, Charlie is standing behind her in the hall. He must see it in my eyes before he shakes his head. I should listen to him. I should heed the warning.

I look back to Maria, and fuck me, I step off the ledge.

"Kane isn't your father."

She doesn't respond. I had no idea how she would react.

I don't look at Charlie, who still stands behind Maria, but I can feel the shock pulsing from him. "King isn't your brother." I add.

She still won't respond, but I see the red that flushes across her chest. I want to touch her but for the first time I'm afraid—I'm afraid of her.

"Mary O'Brien is your mother. She has green eyes and brown hair. She read Dick and Jane to you at bedtime."

Her unblinking eyes stare at me. The red flush climbs up her throat and taints her perfect cheeks.

"You were kidnapped from a zoo at the age of three."

She blinks and looks away from me. She's frowning while shaking her head.

"They still search for you, Maria. They never gave up. I met your mother."

"Stop." She shakes her head while looking at me from the corner of her eye. "Please." Her lips tug down and I see the damage in her eyes as her heart breaks. Maybe she always knew.

"He took you because your real father reneged on a deal. You are meant to marry King."

A choked sob leaves her mouth and she turns away from me. I want to reach for her; I want to hold her, like William once held me as I bled on the ground. The same way she's bleeding now.

"Maria." I call her name and when she looks at me, I have no idea what I want to say.

She shakes her head. "Mary," she says the name and a tear trickles from her unblinking eyes. She holds her head high as if she can hold back the tide of emotion I see battling for release inside her.

"They took me?" The devastation on her face has me caving even further.

"They hid you. Your parents only live a few hours away."

She continues to shake her head and steps back away from me like she can step away from the truth. Her body shakes.

"I didn't know." I need her to believe me. I need her to know I didn't accept this deal with the knowledge that she was stolen.

"Do they know you know?" Charlie asks from behind Maria, and she looks at him now before folding her arms across her chest. I hate how she hunches her shoulders, and steps closer to the stairs. She's trying to protect herself.

"Not now, Charlie." I growl through gritted teeth.

I don't want to look away from Maria. I'm afraid if I do that she will crumble and I won't be able to put her back together.

"Damien, if they know you know, you're as good as dead."

Maria inhales sharply and I cut my gaze to Charlie. "I said not now."

Charlie glares at me and all I want to do is tell him to fuck off. He must read it in my eyes as he turns on his heel and leaves us alone.

"I don't understand." Maria finally says, but I think she does. I think she knows I'm telling her the truth. It's like she's crawling on her knees in hopes that I can stop the truth in her path. The longer we look at each other, the deeper it cuts.

"They can't find out you know," I say before her anger takes away all logic.

Her eyes grow wide and I can already see the hands of the clock moving.

"Maria." I take a step towards her and I'm expecting a slap or for her to tell me to leave. What I don't expect is for her to step towards me and wrap her arms around my waist. I'm frozen for a moment before I wrap my arms around her and she starts to cry.

We stay like this, in her cocoon of pain, and some part of me recognizes this place and finds comfort in the darkness. I don't want the light of acceptance or the shield from the pain. I let it consume her. I let it consume us.

"Mum." The word is said in between bouts of tears, she sobs for a while and then calls out to her mother. I wonder if she is picturing the woman she has spent her whole life looking for. The one she knew existed. I smile painfully into her hair.

"She's real." I reassure her and hold her until she completely exhausts herself.

She grows heavy in my arms as it fully sinks in. I lift her up and hold her to my chest as I climb the stairs. I cradle her as I had once cradled William. Only William's heart had stopped beating. The priests had kicked him until he drew his final breath on a cold concrete ground, on a cold winter's morning, with a stolen peach in his belly. I had crawled to him and pulled him to my chest. My back had still bled, the buckle of the belt had torn chunks of my flesh away. The pain took away my ability to stop them. I had sworn my vengeance on every priest who had worked there.

Each one is as guilty as the next, no one stops it and they remain silent, and that's worse than the crime itself.

I open the double doors and carry Maria to the bed.

I returned a long time later to Melefont and took each of their lives. It was slow and painful. I didn't tell them why, they had no idea why I cut them apart.

They needed an explanation and I refused to give them one.

Laying Maria down, I lie beside her, and pull her into me as she continues to cry for her stolen childhood. I soak up her pain—and roll in it—as I remember William.

We come up for air before being tugged back under the water. A broken part of me doesn't mind drowning with her. The night comes fully in and her cries have stopped but she's awake. Her mind moves too quickly for her to keep up with. I'm not exactly sure how you take in all I just told her.

"They will come for you," I say to the crown of her head. My voice sounds so loud in the silence.

Her hands tighten a bit more around my waist. Her smell consumes me and I close my eyes and inhale. I've already made my decision, I think I made it when I laid eyes on her. That she's mine.

"I won't let them take you." I promise her.

I won't lose another person I love.

CHAPTER TWENTY-FOUR

MARIA

It's been two whole days and I've stayed in the house. Damien hasn't left my side. I keep looking at my phone. Daddy springs up again, and I'm tempted to answer it and ask him if this is real. But it is. I see it each time I look into Damien's eyes.

His fingers entwine with mine as I stare at the TV. I'm not watching what plays out across the screen. Closing my eyes, I allow his warmth to enclose me. It's been chasing away the cold that skims along the outskirts, waiting for its moment to move in and consume me.

"He keeps ringing," I say again, and this time I look at Damien.

"Can you keep your emotions hidden?" He asks.

I exhale. "No." I've never been able to. I've never felt a need to hide anything; which is uncanny since my whole life is a lie. I turn the phone face down. I feel like an imposter. Is my personality even real? I always thought my determination came from my father—Kane. He isn't my father, I remind myself.

For the millionth time I wonder what my actual father looks like. Damien said that they never stopped looking for me. I clench my other hand as I try to imagine twenty-two years of that kind of pain. My stomach lurches at the thought. I keep trying to put Kane and this monster side by side, but it's like having two puzzle pieces that just don't fit. I look up at Damien again and he's watching me.

I'm ready to ask him to lie to me. But that's what it would be, a lie. My phone vibrates again and my chest tightens.

"He won't stay away," I say, looking at the slick back of the phone.

"I know." Damien squeezes our joined hands but doesn't say anything else. It stops ringing and I turn it over. Six missed calls and that's just today. I know Damien put Jack and Mattie on the gates. Charlie hasn't left the house and I know he's hovering close by.

"I'm going for a shower, are you okay here?" Damien slowly untwines our fingers. I nod, not answering him. Will I ever be okay? He gets up and passes me. The screen on the TV becomes my focal point. A monkey swings through the trees, its baby clinging to its stomach. I turn it off and look at my phone again: six missed calls.

I want to ring him back. I want to ask him why. What could he be gaining by keeping me away from my parents? My throat burns and I glance at the sitting-room door, Charlie passes it. No doubt keeping an eye on me so I don't run off.

I get up, feeling naked without Damien. It's odd to rely on someone so much. I leave the living room. Charlie is in the hall. Rome is tucked in his arm. I smile, it feels like a foreign thing to do, but it's hard not to.

"You really got yourself a friend."

He looks down at Rome. "It keeps making noise if I don't hold it."

"She's a clever girl," I say as I step up to Charlie and rub her tiny head. She's cute. I can see myself getting used to her.

I leave Rome and Charlie and climb the stairs. Damien is in the master bedroom's en-suite. I sit on the bed and wait for him to come out. It's weird wanting to be this close to someone. But he offers me sanity. Something I can't seem to find on my own. Lifting up the shirt he just took off, I inhale it and he's here with me—giving me peace. I know the gamble he took for me, I know what he gave up. I just still can't wrap my head around why he did it.

Getting up, I rest his shirt on the bed and make my way into the bathroom. The glass is fogged from the shower. His back is to me as he washes himself. The scars stand out and I want to touch them. Pulling my shirt over my head, he's aware I'm here. His shoulders grow tense, but he doesn't turn around as I take off my clothes.

I open the door and steam pours out. Damien's eyes roam across my body and the green in his eyes darkens with desire.

"I thought you might miss me," I say.

I step up to Damien and I don't ever want that look in his eyes to fade. My core tightens as I lean around him and take the shower gel off the stand. Glancing down, I see his erection growing. Right now I just want this moment to exist, nothing is real beyond this bathroom. I make the decision while I cover my skin with the gel and turn my back on Damien. A zap of electricity goes through my body as he presses himself against me. His large cock is hard against my ass and I move my hips. The hiss from him has me moving again. His hands touch my hips before moving across my stomach, causing the muscles to clench as his hands travel up to my breasts that he palms. I wiggle again against his cock and his teeth graze my ear. "You keeping doing that and I'll have to fuck you up the ass." I can feel the wetness gathering at his words. I move again and one of his hands leaves my breast before trailing down to my pussy.

He separates the flaps before he dips a finger inside. I roll my head back onto his chest and groan. He pushes in another finger and I spread my legs further. He's still palming my breast as my nipples grow harder. I open my eyes, wanting to see him. Turning, he removes his fingers from me. My lips crash against his and my back hits the cold tiles. His erection is heavy on my stomach. I push my tongue into his mouth and groan when he forces his way into my mouth. I'm tempted to bite him, instead I pull him closer.

"Fuck me." I order him and let my head fall back as his lips leave my mouth and trail along my neck. Damien's wicked grin at my order has more juices leaking from me. He bends his head and captures a nipple in his mouth, he sucks it roughly and I bite down on the pain. He releases it quickly and spins me. My cheek is plastered against the cold tiles as he runs his fingers along my ass. "I've been wanting to fuck this from the first day I saw you."

His words have me clenching my thighs. His finger slides into my ass and the sensation has me opening my eyes. His other hand snakes around and touches my clit, enhancing the feeling in my ass. I push out from the wall, giving him access to me. His finger disappears from my ass and the fat head of his cock is pressed against it.

"Your ass is wet for me." Damien's words have me bending over. I want him to fill me. He moves the head of his cock to my pussy and fills it. The movement is instant and has me crying out as I reach for the tiles. He pulls out before slamming back into me. His groan has my own moans growing louder. I won't last long, there is too much built up inside me. I want to grip something, but my hands are flat against the tiles as he pounds into me. I'm so close to my release when he pulls out and doesn't enter me again. I'm ready to ask him why he is stopping when his cock touches my ass and he pushes in slowly until his cock fills my ass. I feel so full, like nothing else could possibly fit in. Damien pulls slowly out of my ass and I'm ready to come.

"Jesus, it's perfect," he says before moving back inside me. "It was made for me."

My body is humming and screaming for release. His words are driving me wild. He bends over me as he fills me again and his hand reaches around and brushes my clit.

"I'm so close." I tell him and he pulls out before pushing harder into me. "Don't come yet." He moves in and out of my ass quicker and I fight with everything not to come. I hold it as he continues to pump into my ass.

"I can't..." I trail off as Damien takes me higher, slamming into my ass. His body tenses and he groans loudly as he pounds my ass and spills his seed in me. I call out my own release and our cries mingle together. Damien removes himself slowly from me and I'm still coming down off the high, my body is all nerve endings and I jump when Damien runs his hand across the bunch of nerves.

"You liked that?"

I push off the wall and turn to him. I feel flushed and sore, but it's perfect. "Yes." His lips capture mine and my hands trail up to his neck. Without breaking the kiss, he moves us under the spray of water. The kiss is different, this one is tender, but it runs deeper. I open my eyes to find

Damien looking at me. He looks gorgeous as the water runs across his wide shoulders and down his chest.

He moves us carefully back to the wall and I don't have to ask what he's doing. His cock is growing again.

"You didn't have enough?" I ask. My body was still humming from my release.

"I'll never have enough of you, Maria." His hungry words surprise me and they don't match the softness of the kiss he places on my lips. I can't stop looking at the softness of his face as he lifts my leg and places his cock at my opening. His eyes flicker up to me. Grabbing my legs, he pulls me up and I wrap them around his waist while coming down onto his cock. It fills me and I cry out again. I feel his slow movements down to the tips of my toes. I love his chest molded against mine. I love our bodies joining together. I love him.

It's like a bolt of lightning through my system as he continues to push in and out of me. The movements grow faster and I look up at him as I moan.

"Let me watch you." His words have me nodding as he rides me faster. His cock stretches me and fills me. The walls of my pussy tighten around him as he moves faster inside me and I can't believe I'm ready to come. This time Damien doesn't stop me, but his eyes never leave my face as I cry out my release. His jaw tightens and he pounds into me before filling me with more of his seed. My body's on fire as he slows his movements and pulls out of me, lowering me back to the ground.

"Damien." I'm moving behind Damien at the sound of Charlie's voice.

"I'm in the shower."

"It's Gerald." Damien's body tenses beside me.

"Give me a moment."

Damien looks down at me and I see the worry in his eyes. "Who's Gerald?" I ask. My heart pounds.

Damien places a kiss on my lips. "Someone who will help us."

Us—like we're a team. Damien gets out and I'm not ready to face the world. I stay under the stream of water as Damien's seed drips from me. I wash myself and my curiosity of who Gerald is has me finally turning off the water and getting out. After drying off, I get dressed into a pair of jeans and a top before heading downstairs. Charlie is in the hall, still holding Rome. She looks so funny in his arms. He won't look at me and I swear there is a red tint on his cheeks. He must have heard me and Damien.

"No need to be embarrassed Charlie," I say. I keep my smirk at bay as he stares at me.

"Where is Damien?" I want to see who Gerald is.

"He won't be long."

I'm ready to protest when Damien steps out of the living room with a tall man beside him. Blue eyes pin me to the spot. Amusement flashes in his eyes. He's in an all-black suit and he steps up to me and offers me his hand.

"You must be Maria." I take his hand, his fingers are soft. He's handsome, but something about him doesn't sit right with me. It's like something moves under his skin. It's almost unsettling.

"You must be Gerald," I say back and he releases my hand.

He glances at Damien and nods. "I'll let myself out." He takes one final look at me before leaving our home.

"He's a little creepy." I wait until he's gone before I speak my mind.

Damien laughs. "That's not normally the reaction Gerald gets from females."

"He's handsome, but still creepy."

I wait for Damien to tell me what they talked about, but he doesn't. "I have to meet someone now, but I won't be long." He places a kiss on my forehead. His hair is still wet from the shower and I run my hands through the strands. He stands still and allows me to do it. "I'll miss you." I tell his hair. I don't filter things, but this new feeling that is rising up inside me is scaring me.

"I won't be long." I meet his smiling eyes and accept the kiss he brushes across my lips.

I release him and let him go. Charlie stays in the hall and Rome yips as Damien walks past her.

"I think she's your bodyguard," I say to Charlie to distract myself as Damien leaves.

"She's very protective." Charlie agrees as he glances down.

"I think I found your soft spot, Charlie."

He dips his chin and shakes his head. "I'm only keeping her quiet."

I smile. "Is that why she doesn't leave your arms?"

I see the ghost of a smile and I want to pump my arm in victory.

"I'm making a coffee, do you want one?"

"Yeah, why not?"

I grab my phone out of the living room to see I have two more missed calls. My stomach churns as reality slowly starts trickling in. Damien asked me if I could control my emotions. As I stare at the ringing phone, I think I might be able to. I press down on the kettle before sliding the green receiver up.

"Maria." It's my father. Hearing his voice has my legs growing weak.

"You're marrying me off again?" My angry words leave my mouth quickly. "How could you!?"

"What did Damien say?" He sounds calm and detached.

I'm shaking my head as I stare at the phone. My eyes and throat burn. "How could you?!" I shout and look up as Charlie steps into the kitchen. He drops Rome who yelps, and he pulls the phone away from my face. I can hear my father's voice and it gets cut off as Charlie ends the call. I don't fight for my phone back, but he hands it to me.

"Just wait until Damien gets back."

I nod my head. He's right. No good could come from hearing my father's words. He isn't my father, a voice reminds me, and my heart cracks a little.

Rome keeps yapping, in her tiny voice. She's prancing around Charlie's ankles.

"He won't be long." Charlie states as he gathers up Rome. My phone rings again and I stare at it before hanging up and stuffing it in the drawer.

"How many sugars?" I ask Charlie and his shoulders relax.

"Two."

I focus on making our coffees as we wait for Damien to return and fix the mess that I had no idea existed before.

So much can change in a moment. I've never understood the power of time, until now. Each second strips away more of the cocoon that Damien has wrapped me in, and the cold that chases me slowly starts to engulf me.

CHAPTER TWENTY-FIVE

DAMIEN

I hate leaving her. I hate walking out the door, but I tell myself it's the last time I'll leave her with this hanging over us. Gerald arriving at my home didn't surprise me. What I asked of him couldn't be discussed over the phone. Jack and Mattie are at the gates and I wave at them as I leave. She has three men around here and I don't intend to stay away long. Once I make this deal with Dean, I can end this.

Gerald had Dean waiting for me at Slane Castle. When I asked Gerald to put me in contact with him, I wasn't sure if he could really pull it off. It felt like a pipe dream, but he managed to make Dean agree to this meeting.

I think of Maria to keep my mind off the meeting. A smile tugs at my lips as I picture her flushed face under the spray of water. She was stunning. I don't think I could ever get use to fucking her. My cock grows now as I think of my cock in her ass. She was built for me. I knew the moment that Kane had smiled at me, and told me I had fulfilled my part of the deal and that it was done; I knew I couldn't let her go. She had somehow gotten under my skin without me noticing. I've always seen her from the moment I was in her home. She always drew my eye, maybe she was always there in my mind without me even knowing.

I push my foot down, not wanting to be away from her for too long. She's still fragile. She is coming to terms with what I told her. She has no idea how strong she really is.

The castle comes into view from the top of the hill as I make my way down the winding driveway. Gerald inherited everything from his grandfather. They had bad blood and Gerald wore his wounds daily. He's a little twisted, but he's fair. I've never had words with Gerald and I hope we can always keep it that way.

I pull up close to the club where I do security. This was once was my playground, but since Maria entered my life, it feels distant—just a filler to a void that never can really be filled.

Locking the car, I make my way into the castle. Gerald had set us up in the house for the meeting. Dean isn't a man you can pick up a phone and ring. You don't find him; he finds you. But after years working in the club, I've seen him several times and that's what prompted me to ask Gerald. If anyone could convince Dean of this meeting, it was Gerald and he turned up trumps.

I enter a large room that holds too many random chairs. My gaze skims across them all until they land on Dean. He's facing an unlit fireplace. I hear the china click as he puts a tea cup down and turns to me.

"Damien." He calls my name like we are friends but this is a first for me.

Dean is the best sniper, and for a fee he will take anyone out, no matter what. He doesn't ask why, just when and where.

But Dean isn't simple.

"Dean," I say his name as I sit down on the hardest looking chair in the room. Straight away I feel his location was intentional. His chair looks soft, a large armchair with lots of padding. Mine is something you would find in an old school.

I sit without pointing out the fucking obvious.

Dark eyes smile at me. Dean's lower face is covered in a thick black beard that he rubs now. "Who's the mark?"

This is the tricky part with Dean. He doesn't hide what he does. When you ask him to take someone out, he tells that person, and offers them to up the bid. Whoever pays him the most gets their way. That's why you don't go near him unless you have enough to make sure you pay your bill.

"The offer I'm making today can't be matched by the other party. So I don't want a negotiation."

He laughs and I know who I'm sitting with. He's a ghost that everyone searches for. I try to keep my tone respectful, but I want the job done quickly without a mess.

"You know, I was settled into retirement. But Gerald called in a favor."

He picks up the small teacup and takes a sip from it. "He must really fucking like you."

I didn't know that he had called in a favor. "I appreciate you meeting me."

His smile leaves his face. "A million a head. I want payment twenty-four hours before the job. I also will pick the meeting spot so I can set up beforehand."

I told Gerald a quarter of a million, that's what I have, but I knew it wouldn't be enough. But a million just isn't possible. "I can't do that." I answer honestly.

He doesn't seem put out. "What you offered is an insult to my profession." He has the power to flex muscle here.

"Dean, a quarter of a million is a lot of money," I say leaning in to him.

"It depends who you are asking. So if you are asking me, I'll tell you it's not."

I clench my jaw. He's a prick. His grin tells me he knows what I am thinking.

"Half a million for both and I need forty-eight hours to get it to you. I'll pick the place."

He runs his hand across his beard again. "One million, thirty-six hours and I still pick the place."

He isn't going to budge and I don't think he's a man who normally negotiates. I hold out my hand. "Deal." I swallow. If I can't get the money, I'm a dead man. He'll hunt me down—and Dean never misses a target.

He takes my hand and laughs as he shakes it. "So who am I marking?"

"You will find that out once the money is sitting in your account." I'm waiting for him to demand their names, but he shrugs.

"Fine. Be a stubborn prick." His grin softens the blow of his words. He stands up. "Nice doing business with you." I stand and shake on it.

"Don't keep me waiting." He tightens his hold on my hand, crushing my fingers. I don't flinch as he releases my hand and walks from the room while whistling.

I know that I need to make sure I get the money or I'm a dead man. You don't approach Dean with a few grand. He only deals in high numbers, but he gets the job done. It's clean and untraceable.

Before he can leave, the door opens and Gerald steps in. Dean takes his hand and pulls him in before turning to me. "This motherfucker here is a God."

"The club is ace." He tells Gerald while releasing him.

"A pleasure having you here, Dean." Gerald seems fond of him and I approach them.

Dean points at Gerald. "It's a good thing Gerald isn't a sniper." Dean mimics holding a gun while closing one eye. "He'd be picking them off one at a time." He laughs and so does Gerald. I force a smile but I need to leave. I need time to get the money.

"Pow, pow, pow." Dean laughs as he pretends to kill people. He's a psycho.

"I don't need a gun." Gerald says lazily back to him.

"I better be going." I don't want to hear all their dirty secrets.

"Yeah, get me my money." Dean nods and if I didn't need him, I'd punch him in his arrogant fucking face.

I nod at him before thanking Gerald and I'm out the door. The next part of my plan will be so much harder than the first. It's a point of no return.

CHAPTER TWENTY-SIX

MARIA

Damien has been gone most of the day. I finish eating a quarter of the sandwich that I made for me and Charlie. My stomach still hasn't fully settled and I'm finding it hard to swallow the food.

"Are you not eating yours?" He points to my plate and I slide it across to him. Charlie picks it up and starts eating. Taking his empty plate and my mug into the kitchen, my heart plummets into my feet.

Nate's at the back door, staring in at me. I glance over my shoulder. "You want another cup of tea?" I shout in to Charlie.

"Yeah." His answer sounds distracted and I know he's still caught up in the show he was watching. I flick on the kettle before walking to the double back doors. Opening one, I slip out. Nate stands back.

"What are you doing here?" I whisper to him. It's cold outside and I fold my arms across my chest. He's wearing a t-shirt and I don't know how he isn't freezing. He stuffs his hands into his jeans pockets.

"I want to make sure you're okay."

I glance back into the kitchen to make sure Charlie doesn't arrive. I've always liked Nate, so I don't want him in trouble. "Yeah. Why wouldn't I be?" He didn't know about my family, so his concern has me frowning at him.

"I know how he treats you."

I laugh. I want to point out that it began a million years ago, and that I love Damien. But the set of his jaw has me keeping that information hidden.

"He's good to me now. You need to go." I have no idea how he got on the property with Jack and Mattie on the gates, but it doesn't matter. All that matters right now is that he leaves before Charlie comes out.

"Nate, seriously you need to go." He's staring at me and it's creeping me out a bit.

"Okay." He nods his head but doesn't leave. He's staring at me again and it's unsettling.

I pull open the door, seeking the warmth of the house. A cloth covers my mouth and I try to pull away from Nate.

"I'm sorry." His words are whispered into my ear as I try to kick and claw my way out of his arms. My movements are too slow and sluggish and I stop. With one arm around me, Nate half carries and half drags me.

"Please." The word is slurred and I hate how numb I feel but my mind is sharp. "What did you give to me?"

He doesn't answer, or maybe he can't hear me. "Please." I beg again and his hand around my waist tightens as he pulls me along the side of the house. We don't move to the front before a small gate covered with shrubbery opens. A car door opens and he places me in it.

"King." His name tumbles from my mouth. His lip tugs up into a smirk.

"Welcome home." Nate climbs in beside me and the car pulls away from the curb, away from my home, away from Damien.

I keep conscious the whole time. I nearly wish my mind was as numb as my body right now.

"I told them how he was mistreating you," Nate says.

I can't move my head to look at him. "Moron," I mumble, and from King's laughter, my word is understandable.

"Nate was so worried about you." King reaches down and pushes hair out of my face. "So was I." I recoil from his touch.

"You're sick."

"He messed with her head." Nate's words come from my left. The car shifts under us as it speeds up.

"Where are we going?" Nate asks.

There is a sharp noise and my stomach tightens at the odd sound. Nate hits the floor and his lifeless eyes look up at me. I'm trying to move, trying to get away but I can't move. A distorted sob falls from my lips and the world shifts as King sits me up. He holds my arms and he's too close.

Tears leak from my eyes.

"Why are you so upset?" I hate how his eyes trail across my face. Has he always looked at me like this? I feel sick.

"Damien," I say his name.

King's face tightens. "He has signed you back over. He doesn't want you anymore."

Liar. "You will marry someone else."

"Who?" I swallow the bile that threatens to claw up my throat. It's there in his eyes.

"Me."

"You're my brother." My words are so unclear and the frustration is making them incoherent.

"No I'm not. So it's okay." He smiles and now I think back to our childhood. He never had a girlfriend. I know he liked women but he never kept them around.

I swallow the saliva in my mouth. "You're sick."

He frowns. "Maria, I'm not your brother. I've always been here for you." The car slows down and King gets out when it comes to a stop. My skin crawls when he reaches back and places an arm under my legs, the other arm wraps around my waist as he cradles me to his chest. My stomach roils and I try to calm my pounding heart. I look around as he carries me into the house. We are home.

"Why is there blood dripping out of the car?" My father asks King the moment we step into the room. I want to ask him to stop this madness, but he looks over me like I'm not fucking drugged.

"Nate was being awkward." King places me on the couch and my father looks at me.

Tears spring to my eyes. "Daddy." My lip trembles. I want this to stop. This is insane.

"What did you say to her?" He asks King as he sits beside me.

"The truth. That she's not my sister and we are marrying."

My father kneels down. "I would have said it gentler." He brushes the hair off my face and I try to move back.

"You have nothing to fear." He tells me, and for a moment I believe him. Nothing can harm me. The image of him blurs.

"Please." I don't know what I'm asking for. For him to tell me the truth, for him to apologize for taking me.

My mother steps into the room and she's as dismissive of me as always. All I can think of is that I'm some other woman's baby. It makes sense of how she looks at King, like he's her world.

"Now it shouldn't have to come to this. It's actually simple. Damien has signed off on the divorce and you can marry King. Marrying Damien was a precaution." He rises. "One I'm glad I took."

"Precaution?" I mumble and my mother glares at me.

"Kane, she's drooling on the couch."

"You should be nicer to her, she will be your daughter-in-law." King speaks before placing a kiss on her cheek. I want to run away as he steps up to me.

"I know this all seems weird. But we can go away for a while. Just you and me."

A whimper of disgust leaves my mouth.

"I don't like this Kane."

I'm nodding at my mother. I agree with her.

He stands up now. "You knew this would happen."

I move my body and am surprised when it obeys. I'm not delighted when I hit the ground hard like a sack of spuds. My chin takes the impact and a metallic taste fills my mouth. King drags me off the floor and I land on the couch.

"Look at your fucking face." He grips my chin, rotating my head.

"Language." I'm glaring past King to my mother as she corrects King.

I close my eyes against the onslaught of anger that wants to take over. Who are these people? I've always felt detached from them, but right now I'm looking at a bunch of strangers.

King leaves and I'm staring at my father, or the man who is pretending to be him. "You've always been headstrong. You get that from me." He smiles fondly at me and right now if I could, I'd spit in his face.

King arrives back in with a cloth. I sink into the couch as far as I can. "Don't be awkward." He warns me as he grips the back of my head.

"King." I plead with the man who has been my brother my whole life. The one who has protected me. The one who has always made me laugh.

King cleans my face before his eyes meet mine. "I know this all seems crazy. Trust me, when I found out at fourteen that I would marry you, it wasn't easy to accept." He touches my face and I pull away from him.

"Don't fucking touch me."

"She needs to wash her mouth out." My fake mother says.

"Maria, I know it's confusing." My father sits down across from me and King moves away to let him speak to me. "You are the daughter of my best friend."

I want to scream that I know. But I keep my mouth shut.

"I was your godfather."

My stomach twists and I keep a track on King's movements. Each time I look at him, I see the wheels spinning in his head. How had I not seen it before? I wasn't looking for it.

"He died and I took you in."

"We fed, clothed, and educated you." My mother starts knocking off shit on her fingers.

"You didn't love me." My words aren't as slurred. The drugs are finally wearing off.

"How could I? You aren't mine. I never hurt you." She defends herself.

"I should have told you this sooner, but you fell into the role of my daughter." The truth was always somewhere in the middle.

"My mother?" I ask as I picture the woman with the green eyes and brown hair.

"She died too."

Tears spring to my eyes. He is such a good liar. So good that I could never have known.

"What was her name?" I ask as tears spill.

"Marcella."

"What a horrible name," I say.

He smiles.

"Mary sounds nicer," I say.

He pales and glances at King. "You said he didn't know."

King snaps his attention to me. "He doesn't know."

"Mary O'Brien." I shout her name and my fake mother runs to shut the sitting-room door like it will keep the secret in.

"YOU. STOLE. ME." I shout at the top of my lungs, unable to keep it in any longer. Kane gets up and the rage that he displays on his face would sink a fucking ship. But I'm already losing, I'm already drowning.

"YOU. STOLE. ME." I roar again.

"Shh." My fake mother clamps a hand across my mouth, and I've never been so happy to have her hands on me as I sink my teeth in. She screams pulling it away but I don't release her. Her other hand strikes my face repeatedly until I let her go.

"Jesus Christ!" Kane shouts and everyone freezes. I can feel the warm liquid drip from my chin.

"You are a kidnapper! You sick fuck!" I shout at him.

His face tightens and he steps up to me.

"Hit me." I dare him. I want him to. What I don't expect is for King to stand in front of me.

"Everyone, calm down, we can figure this out."

"She knows who she is. Are you stupid? She can go to the police." Kane's panicked voice should be terrifying me. But all I can do is laugh as I watch his stupid plan go down the drain.

"Were you that desperate for King to have a bride that you kidnapped me, raised me and married me off to Damien before taking me back?" I can't make sense of the stupidity of this.

"Be quiet, Maria." King looks at me over his shoulder and I try to kick out at him but my foot barely moves.

"No. How about fuck you?" He spins and bends down so he's facing me. "You're not helping yourself."

"What? You are helping me? The same way you helped Nate?" Nate's dead eyes stare up at me and I should have far more reason to stay quiet but I can't. I can't stay quiet as the people who took everything from me are standing right here.

CHAPTER TWENTY-SEVEN

DAMIEN

I'm on my way back when my phone rings. Charlie's name flashes up on the screen.

"Is she giving you trouble?" I grin at the phone. It's starting to get dark. I honestly thought they'd have rung me sooner, wondering what's taking me so long.

"Damien, she's missing."

I turn on the wipers as the rain starts to fall. "What do you mean, missing?" I grip the steering wheel. If he's ringing, that means that no one came in and took her.

"Jack and Mattie said no one came in or out. But I've searched the house and she isn't here."

My body relaxes. "Check again. It's not that big of a house."

"Damien, it's been hours."

Worry starts to creep in. "And you're only ringing me now?"

"I thought she was hiding, or went off to the shops. But her car, phone, and purse are here."

"Fuck!" I slam my hands against the steering wheel. "They took her."

"No one came into the house."

I cut off Charlie. "King. It's King. He had left photos in the house before. He must have a key. He found a way not to use the front gate. Check outside, I'm on my way." I hang up and push the pedal to the floor.

I hit King's number and my heart pounds as it continues to ring out. His voice message fills my car and I end the call before hitting the redial button.

"What?" His answer is quick and harsh.

"You have her?" I ask, but I already know.

"Who?" I can hear the laughter in the fuckers voice.

"If you touch her..."

His laughter rings down the phone. "She's to be my wife."

"I've had her, but you know that already."

Silence vibrates down the phone and I smirk. "You followed us to Rome. You're a sick fuck, King."

"I knew you fucked her. No worries. I can still enjoy her."

I grip the steering wheel tightly. "I'll buy her off you."

His laughter is louder, but he settles down. "How much?"

I didn't expect him to bite. "Two million."

"Now, where are you going to get two million from?"

"Does it fucking matter?" I growl down the phone.

The wipers move at full speed, barely keeping the water off the windshield.

"I'll pass." His answer has me ready to offer more, but the motherfucker hangs up on me.

I dial Charlie's number. "It's King, he has her."

"Yeah, Nate's body was just dumped at your gate. It's a warning to stay away."

My heart pounds in my chest.

"Damien..."

I hang up on Charlie. I know what he is going to suggest. But I won't forget Maria. I can't.

This messes up everything. I had imagined meeting Kane and King and having Dean clip them. Maria should have been safe behind the large gate and safe with Charlie.

I hit the steering wheel again. Fuck. I am so fucked.

I can't push the car any faster as I tear down the road. I have no choice. There is only one other person I can try to reason with.

I'm waiting for ten minutes. Each time I look at the clock on the phone, my heart beats heavier. He isn't coming. I'm ready to call Charlie when his car rolls up. I get out and he turns off his engine. His eyes bore into me as he climbs out of the car.

"I hear you made quite the offer." Kane doesn't smile as he climbs out of his car. We've met on mutual ground. I would have had Dean here to kill him, but Dean worked on a fucking schedule and didn't do short notice.

"Two million."

He shakes his head. "It's not enough."

He was talking, that was a good sign.

"Is she okay?"

"I didn't know you cared so much, Damien." Kane stands taller.

"Now you know."

He grins. "I'm not buying it. I know you are aware of who she is, so you must know her worth. Two million is pennies."

"You think I'm buying her because she's worth more?"

Kane raises both eyebrows. "We are businessmen. Maybe we can come to some sort of arrangement."

"Like what?"

"You can have her back after King has her for two years. You keep her identity to yourself and you get to stay alive."

I'm shaking my head and stuff my hands into my pockets so I don't strangle him. "Why two years?"

"She's not dead, Damien. She is the heir to the O'Brien wealth, at the age of twenty five."

I feel sick. No wonder he took her and kept her. She's worth billions.

"I've invested money and time into her. It was a long term investment that will pay off now."

It's my turn to smile at him. "That's where you fucked up, Kane. Her parents know she's alive. I've just come from there."

"You wouldn't be so fucking stupid." His eyes are wide and he shakes his head.

"I wouldn't say stupid. I'd say desperate, just like them. They will give anything to have her back. Take the two million and walk away."

He tries to reel in his anger, but he struggles. "I should put a bullet in your fucking head."

"They know I'm here. They know you have her. They are remaining silent. It would be wise if you give her back. Two million will be paid to you."

Kane turns away from me and I see the information sink in. He shakes his head. "I'll take her far away. They'll never find her again."

My stomach twists. "So, what? Do you run for the rest of your life? Or, you take two million and walk away?"

"I want sixty million."

I laugh this time. Greedy bastard. "They are asset rich, not money rich. So take the money, Kane."

He glares at me from the corner of his eye. "Maybe slicing her fucking throat would be more fun than two million."

He pulls his gun on me and I take a step back while raising my hands.

"I trusted you." His temper flairs. "You had to fucking dig."

"I was only doing what I would have any other time. If King hadn't killed Andrew, I wouldn't have been suspicious."

"I respected you." He wiggles the gun closer to me.

"They know I'm here." I remind him. I've never gone up against Kane before. I've never had to. But he's trigger happy.

He's beyond pissed and I don't blame him. I had no idea she would inherit it all at the age of twenty-five. It explains why he wants her back now.

"Andrew's not the first to discover who she is. That's why I had you marry her, to throw those fuckers off the scent."

"At the firm that King works at?"

Kane grins. "You really did your homework. You didn't have to double cross me."

"I didn't. Maybe if you told me the truth at the start, it wouldn't have come to this."

Kane turns away from me and my heart pounds. "Two million is bullshit." He glares at me.

"Tell Larry I want ten." They would give everything for her. "It's nowhere near her fucking worth."

Kane's temper flares again and he's back to wiggling the gun. "Did you sleep with her?"

"I don't see how that matters now." I say.

The gun fires and I duck. Looking up at Kane, he still holds the gun in the air. "It does matter, to King."

"Yes. I did sleep with her." I rise slowly but keep my hands up.

"After I told you not to."

I know I'm a marked man. If I don't kill Kane first, he will kill me. But right now, he needs me. I'm the link to his money.

"Do we have a deal?" I ask.

"No, we don't."

My stomach plummets.

"I want Larry and Mary to give me ten million. I want them to look at the man who took their daughter. That will be a hard lesson for Larry to learn."

"Don't you think that's a bit sick?" I ask.

He grins. "If this is what it boils down to. I won't cower. I want him to know it was me, and what better way, than doing it while he's handing me over the money."

"Where?" I ask.

"I'll be in contact."

I don't want him to go. I won't know if she's safe. "She can't be harmed." I call after Kane.

He pauses at the car.

"Says who?"

"Says me." I call back.

He grins and climbs into the car. I don't move until he drives away.

I try to stay calm as I walk to the car. Opening the door, I slide my phone out and dial Charlie's number. "Please, tell me you have her?"

CHAPTER TWENTY-EIGHT

MARIA

I've been left in the sitting room alone. My fake mother is nursing her wounds. What a bitch. I wiggle my foot and pins and needles erupt. I need to get out of here; I need to get to the police. My head snaps up as the sitting-room door opens and King steps in with a basin of water. His eyes clash with mine and my insides quiver.

"Don't fucking touch me," I bark at him.

He rolls his eyes before sitting down. "I'm still King." He speaks while wetting the cloth.

"You're a fraud."

His eyes snap up to mine, the corners grow tight and I'm waiting for his anger but instead he cleans the blood from my face. I move continuously until he grips my chin and holds me still.

"I know it's weird."

He starts and I'm trying to pull my face out of his hands. "Weird? It's twisted."

"You always were a drama queen. We aren't siblings." He ignores me and tightens his grip on my face, keeping me still.

"Was there ever, at a stage, where you felt guilty?" I ask.

His eyes flicker up to mine and he lets my face go. "Yes. I feel bad about how mam treats you. I've asked her to be nicer."

"What about knowing my whole life is a lie? What about my real parents? What about knowing you're pretending to be my brother?"

He won't look at me now.

"King. We grew up together. I don't understand." I shake my head as my body quivers for a different reason. The deceit is too deep.

"I always kept you safe." He pleads with me to understand.

"I needed someone to keep me safe from you." I kick out and he's not expecting it, he falls back, knocking over the water. I kick air the second time.

His face hardens when he looks up at me. I'm waiting for a blow, but he rights himself and sits up on the couch beside me. My skin crawls.

I'm trying to angle myself away from him.

"I've never harmed you."

I glance at him from the corner of my eye. I want to laugh. I want to tell him how fucking wrong he is. "What do you think you are doing now?"

The door opens and Rita steps in. I can't even label her mother, or fake mother. She's worse than them. She's a mother. She holds her bandaged hand high. Her eyes dart from the spilt water and back to King.

"Ma, it's fine." King starts while clenching his jaw.

She shakes her head. "I didn't want you involved with this." She doesn't hide her disgust as she stares at me.

"There is a special place in hell for a bitch like you," I announce.

She steps into the room.

"Ma. Just leave. Give us a minute."

I try to move away from King. A minute for what? Rita glares at me before closing the sitting-room door.

King turns to me. "Why are you provoking her?"

My chest feels tight and I look away from him. There is too much spinning inside me and I've never wanted to lash out so much. I don't even want to escape. I want to stay here and hurt them so badly. My words aren't enough.

Silence stretches out as I stare at the wall.

"I know you let him touch you."

My head snaps to King and I'm ready to throw up. "If you put your fucking hands on me!" My heart pings around in my chest. He flinches like I've hurt him. I will, I will tear his eyes out if he tries a thing. I will fight with every breath in my body.

His fists tighten and I don't look away from the hate that has started to burn in his eyes.

"You turn my stomach." I turn away from him.

His fingers dig painfully into my face as he drags my gaze back to his. "Is it the scar?" He squeezes my face painfully.

I force a laugh out. "The scar is the only nice thing on your face."

He lets my face go and it burns. "You'll come around." He's trying to convince himself that this somehow will work out.

"It was your fault." He points at the scar and I want to punch him in the mouth.

"Remember you wanted me to play with you on the bunk beds."

I look away from him and the stupid memory that's tainted now.

"I fell down the side and split my face open."

"A pity you didn't bleed out," I say as the door opens again. My body goes stiff as Kane fills the door.

"I'm stepping out, I shouldn't be more than an hour."

"Where are you going?" King asks.

"A loose end I need to tie up." Kane smiles at King and something passes between the men.

My heart pounds. A loose end? "Keep her quiet until I get back." Kane won't look at me and I'm left once again with King.

"What loose end?" I ask King the moment the door closes. His smile leaves his face as he turns to me.

"Is it Damien?" My heart pounds faster.

King just stares at me. I hear the front door close as Kane leaves. Is he going to hurt Damien?

"King!" I shout his name. "Tell me!"

"One minute you want to hurt me, the next you want me to tell you things." He's looking at me but I don't feel like he's fully present.

You can do this, Maria. I try to relax my shoulders. "I'm being too hard on you. I know you're the only one who has ever been nice to me." I shrug and notice I have more power in my body. It feels like a numb foot, but it's slowly coming back.

208

King still doesn't speak. I want to smack him in the face. "I'm scared," I say and look away from him. "I'm sorry about your lip." I add and take a peek at him.

He's smiling. His smile turns into laughter that rings out around the sitting room.

"Is this you trying to act nice?" His laughter dies down. "I should really let you continue and see if you try to seduce me." He's grinning and I try to swing my arm but he grips it easily, I'm not fast enough. "Your eyes are burning with hatred. I know you. I know every part of you." He throws my hand back at me with anger.

"Where is Kane going?" I start again.

"To kill Damien." King doesn't smile, but his eyes drink up my fear.

"No!" I'm shaking my head like I might be able to push the fear down. "King, you can't let that happen!"

"I hate him." His eyes roam across me. "I hate that he touched what is mine."

I try to lean away from him again. Everything in me becomes uncomfortable. This is like watching a sex scene with your parents, only a thousand times worse.

Noise from the kitchen has us both looking at the door. "That mad bitch Rita must be having a fit," I say.

King fires me a warning look as the noise stops. "Stay here."

"No, I was just about to take a jog." I fire back and hate the laughter I see in King's eyes before he leaves. I don't wait, I throw my body onto the floor. I'm faster this time and turn my face sideways so my cheek takes the impact. It still hurts. My arms have more strength in them than I expected and I grip the carpet before pulling my body along the floor. Pure elation tears through me as I move. There is more noise coming from the kitchen. It sounds like someone is fighting. Loud voices have me freezing.

"Help!" I roar at the top of my lungs. "Help me!"

My heart bounces in my chest as the door swings open and King fills the doorway. A whimper leaves my lips. No!

A roar has me opening my eyes as King is forced into the room by Charlie. "Charlie." His name falls from my lips and I'm ready to cry with relief.

Charlie charges at King, he's so much bigger, his body slams into King's stomach and he drives both of them across the couch. I glance back at the sitting-room door and keep crawling to freedom.

Charlie's roar of pain has me freezing, I turn and try to see what's happening but they are still behind the couch. Everything goes still.

Go! Go!

I drag myself until half my body is in the hall. A hand touches my waist and I'm ready to cry. Glancing over my shoulder. Charlie picks me up. He cries out but manages to get me off the ground.

We are moving into the kitchen where Rita lies on the ground. I'm not sure if she's dead. I hope she is.

Charlie half-walks, half-runs with me. Sweat soaks his face and he starts to look a little gray.

"You're hurt, put me down."

He looks down at me; his eyes are swimming with pain. "Can you walk?" He asks me.

I know I can't. I shake my head and he keeps walking. "Charlie stop. We can rest." I'm not sure where, but he isn't looking well at all.

Charlie doesn't heed my words. His steps are slowing and he leans against a wall. I'm glancing back at the house. I can still see it. "Did you bring a car?" I ask him, my panic of King coming out has my heart pounding.

"Yeah." He pushes off the wall and starts walking again.

"Where is Rome?"

Charlie's eyes flicker to me, he blinks trying to concentrate.

"You better not have left her on her own, Charlie." I bite each word.

"I'm sorry Maria, I had no choice."

"She won't be happy." I'm talking shit. I look over Charlie's shoulder expecting to see Rita or King, but the path behind us is clear.

"Is he dead?" I ask Charlie.

"No." Charlie's words make him move faster.

When he slows down and lowers me, I turn and look at the blue car. Charlie slides me into the front seat. His torso is red with blood. "We need to get you to a hospital."

He closes the door and clings to the car as he makes his way around to the driver side. He's not going to make it.

He does. I don't know how, but Charlie manages to pull himself into the car and start it.

I glance out the window back at the house and it disappears as Charlie starts to drive.

"Charlie." He leans over the steering wheel, the car veering into the ditch. I reach across and nearly fall on top of him as I pull the steering wheel, bringing us back on the road.

"Charlie!" I shout his name and he sits up.

"You need a hospital." He's losing too much blood.

He tries to stay alert but his face grows grayer by the second. A phone rings and he sits up straighter, blinking.

"It's in my pocket." Charlie tells me. My fucking hands are like rubber as I fight to get the phone out. I manage to and I can't even tell If I have a tight grip or not.

"Please tell me you have her?"

Damien's voice has a strangled cry leaving my mouth. "I'm here!" I cry into the phone. "I'm here!"

CHAPTER TWENTY-NINE

DAMIEN

I find them parked on the side of the road. All I want to do is take Maria in my arms but her eyes are so wide as she stares at all the blood that oozes out of Charlie's side.

"He won't stop bleeding." Her hands push down on his side, tears fill her eyes. I try not to count all the marks on her face.

Charlie groans and I pull him out of the driver side. He's fucking heavy as I drag him into the back of the car. Maria gets out and closes the door. She holds onto the car as she tries to walk around to me. Her movements are sluggish and make me work quicker as I get Charlie into the back and close the door. I turn to Maria and grip her before she falls.

"What's wrong?" I can't look away from all the red marks on her face. It looks like someone slapped her.

"They drugged me." She keeps pushing towards the car and I get her in and close the door.

I can't think straight as I pull out and drive. I keep glancing at Maria, but each time I can't bring myself to ask her what happened.

She curls herself up in the front seat and stares out the window. I force my foot heavier on the peddle and focus on Charlie.

"Charlie, are you with us?"

He groans. He's losing too much blood. I keep rotating from looking at Maria, glancing in the rearview mirror at Charlie, and watching the road. The sign for the hospital is up ahead. I pull up outside the door.

"Maria, come with me." I can't leave her in the car. She nods and I see her struggle to open the door. I get out and she has the door open.

Charlie seems heavier. "Stay with us, Charlie," I say as I wrap my arm around him. I slow as Maria catches up to me. She wraps her arms around her waist. I want to touch her so badly.

The moment we step into the emergency room, the receptionist calls for help. Charlie's taken from my arms and rushed from the room. A nurse asks me questions about what happened, but I have no clue.

"It was a bar fight. He was stabbed," I say. It looked like a stab wound.

I glance back and Maria is standing behind me. I reach back and entwine her fingers pulling her into my side. The nurse looks at her and frowns.

"Were you in the fight too?"

The nurse glances at me with suspicion. I don't blame her. Maria looks terrified and the marks on her face look like she's been manhandled.

"No." Maria speaks up and glances at me.

"Let the nurse take a look at you."

Maria grips my hand tighter.

"I won't leave you." I reassure her.

The nurse doesn't look happy that I'm not leaving. She leads us to an exam station.

"Was there anyone else injured at the bar?" She asks while taking out disinfectant wipes.

She's speaking to Maria and not me.

"No." Maria doesn't sound so sure.

"Why don't you sit up on the bed and I'll take a look at your face."

"My face is fine." Maria fires quickly and I squeeze her hand.

"Let her take a look." I help Maria up on the bed. Her steps are still unsteady.

"Are you feeling weak?" The nurse asks as she starts to clean blood off the side of Maria's neck. My heart pounds. I hadn't seen the blood before.

"Yeah, I forgot to eat today."

The nurse cleans the blood off. "This isn't your blood."

Maria's eyes flick to me. "It must be Charlie's," she says.

"Could we have a moment?" The nurse asks me and I'm not ready to leave Maria. I can see the wheels turning in the nurse's head. She thinks the marks on Maria are from me.

I nod. "I'll be outside." I can check on Charlie. I lean in and place a kiss on Maria's forehead. It's not enough. I want to hold her. I want to know what happened, but for now, it has to be enough.

No one has any information on Charlie. He's in surgery, that's all I'm being told. It was King who did it. The same stab wound that Andrew had.

I exhale loudly as I wait for the nurse to let me back into Maria. When she does, I feel nervous to be finally alone with her.

She's sitting on the bed, looking at her hands. She's a picture sitting in the white cubicle. I hate the haunted look in her eyes when she notices me standing by the curtain.

"I thought Kane killed you." Her words are said on a trembling lip. I walk to her and pull her into my chest and she grips me. She doesn't cry like I expect.

"They are sick," she says, her words are fueled with so much fucking anger.

"King ..." She trails off and I pull her closer.

I want to ask her if he touched her but I can't. I close my eyes to the marks on her face.

"He's the one I'm being married off to."

I swallow and hold her tighter. "It's okay. He won't get near you again."

"He wants to marry me."

I let her go and try to calm her. Her heart is racing so fast. "It's over. You're safe."

She's shaking her head. "He knows who I am."

I'm nodding. "Maria, it's okay."

Her mouth opens and closes. Her hands grip my face. "Kiss me," she demands, and I do.

I place my lips on hers and give her all of me. I'd give it all up for her, and I am. Her kiss is panicked and hungry and I try to slow it down.

"Are you trying to get us kicked out?"

She laughs and kisses my bottom lip. "How's Charlie?"

I exhale again. "I don't know. He's in surgery but we have to go. We can't stay here."

"Kane?"

I nod. "Is King dead?" I don't want him to be. I want to be there when Dean puts a bullet between his eyes.

"I don't know." Maria shrugs and her eyes waver. I hug her again. "Did he touch you?" I ask what I fear the most.

I lean out and she wraps her arms around her waist. "No."

Relief has me relaxing. I can't look away from the marks on her face. "Rita hit me."

Kane's wife. I have a mind to add her to the list with Dean. I nod, as of right now anger races through me.

"But otherwise no one hurt me." She shrugs. "They said you gave me back." Her voice wobbles.

I grip her face gently and make her look at me. "Never."

A tear trickles from her eye. "I know I'm not easy."

I kiss her lips, stopping the words. "You are perfect, Maria. Don't ever change."

We need to leave. "Your parents know you're alive."

The remaining color bleaches from her face. "My parents?"

There is such a childlike look in her eyes and I want to hurt Kane so bad for what he has done.

"I'm taking you to them."

Her mouth opens and she sucks in air. "Now?"

The smile on her face has me smiling. "Yes."

Her face falls. "I can't."

"Why?" What was she so afraid of?

"I need to change first. I'm a mess."

I laugh. "Maria..."

She holds up her hands. "No Damien, I want a shower." Mattie and Jack are still at the house, but Kane and King will be beyond angry that she's missing. I can't risk it.

"Okay."

She smiles and I see some of Maria back in her eyes. I call the nurse and she clears Maria to leave. Charlie is still in surgery. But I will check back later.

We leave and Maria grows quiet in the car again. I pass the house and she glances back at the road.

"Damien what are you doing?"

I take a quick look at her. "You're not going back. Kane will be looking for you."

"I can't meet my parents looking like this." The desperation in her eyes has my chest tightening.

"Your parents won't care what you are wearing."

"I do. Now turn the car around."

I keep going. "No."

"I need to get Rome."

I suppress a smile. "Jack has Rome."

"Rome doesn't even know Jack."

This time I can't stop the grin that tugs at my lips. It dies quickly as Maria grabs the steering wheel.

"Are you fucking crazy?" I straighten the car back on the road. My heart pounds heavily in my chest. "Maria?" I want an explanation for why she just tried to fucking kill us.

"I don't want to meet them." She looks at me and I take a calming breath before slowing the car down and pulling over to the side of the road. I don't turn off the engine as I turn to Maria.

"It's scary," I say.

She doesn't answer.

"Doesn't mean you can pull the fucking steering wheel out of my hands."

"Don't curse at me." Her eyes grow wide.

I'd kick anyone else out. "You are lucky I love you, Maria."

She freezes and her chest stops moving as she stares at me. "You are lucky I love you, too, or I'd slap you for speaking to me like that."

I'm grinning as I lean over and grab her face. "You love me?" I ask her because I want to hear her say it again.

"Maybe, like a little." She teases and I see the ghost of a smile on her face.

"Liar." I declare before kissing her. Her lips move under mine and she's so fucking perfect. Her hands grip my shoulders and my cock grows instantly hard.

I break the kiss reluctantly, but I don't release her face so she's looking at me. "They are going to love you." She tries to pull away, but I hold her face in my hands. "You are perfect, Maria." She needs to believe it.

Her nostrils flair and when she nods her head in agreement, I finally let her go. She doesn't try to pull the steering wheel out of my hands again as we continue the drive to her parents' house. My stomach twists when I think of her meeting them for the first time. I'm nervous for her. My phone buzzes, I don't have it in the dock. I've been waiting on a call from Kane, calling me out on betraying him again. King's name flashes up on the screen. I glance at Maria and she's focused out window. I turn the phone upside down so she can't see who's ringing.

"I hope Charlie will be okay." She's biting her nails. A trait I've never seen her do before.

"It'll take a lot more to get rid of Charlie."

Maria narrows her eyes playfully at me before they fill with worry.

"You know he survived a war in his own country. He's crashed three cars, been in too many fights to count. He even survived working for me. I'm sure he'll be fine."

"He better be." Maria's voice has my jealousy rising.

I look at her.

"Who'll take care of Rome?"

I grin. "I'll have her put down."

Maria's hand strikes my arm. "You can't do shit like that, Maria, not when I'm driving."

She shrugs. "Then don't threaten my dog's life."

We are close to her parent's estate. I glance at her. She has no idea who she is and soon she'll find out.

Soon she's going to realize she's already a billionaire—that she's an only child, and that her parents never stopped searching for her.

I know it will be bitter sweet.

CHAPTER THIRTY

DAMIEN

We pull up outside the O' Brien residence. I don't get a chance to turn the car off when the front door opens and Mary comes running out. Jesus. Maria doesn't get a second to brace herself.

"This is your mother." I get to say.

"I remember her."

The door is pulled open and Mary is gushing. "Maria." She's touching her hair and face. "My Maria."

I look away and see her father, Larry, standing at the door. Something so broken reflects in his eyes as he watches his wife hold their daughter. Twenty-three years is too many years to lose in a lifetime. I hate that I can't reverse the clock.

"Oh, my baby." I don't look as Mary still clings to Maria. Larry finally comes down the steps. His eyes meet mine and he nods before walking around to the passenger side of the car.

"Mary, let her breathe." Larry tries to pull his wife off Maria.

"Thank you." Mary's eyes collide with mine and I can't speak. There is so much gratitude there that I can't breathe.

"Thank you." Tears stream down her face.

"Let's go in and sit down." Larry holds his wife, but her eyes are trained on Maria. She's gripped her hands as if she is stopping herself for reaching out to Maria.

"That sounds good," I say to Larry while turning off the car. Maria glances at me and she is a pillar of strength. I lean in and brush a kiss on her lips. I'm so proud of her. Larry moves Mary back and allows Maria out of the car.

Maria wraps an arm around her mother's shoulders. Instead of the pain I thought I would see, I see wonder as she looks at the woman she remembers. She's fucking amazing.

"I'll be with you in a minute. You go ahead."

Maria pauses, but I smile and she nods. "Don't take long."

I grin at her. Always with a demand. I wait until she goes inside before taking out my phone. King has rung several times. I look up at the house, as if I can see inside it and the heartbreak that he and his father caused.

"What?"

"How's Charlie?" He starts out with.

"You're horribly fucking stupid," I say.

I move the phone away from my ear as he roars his death threats down the phone. I wait, looking back up at the house. I don't need any more fuel to want him dead, but I take more.

"What do you want?" I say once he's calmed down.

"I want Maria back."

I hang up. My heart pounds. I'm playing with fire. But fuck me, I'm ready to get burned.

It rings and I answer.

"You hang up on me again..." King starts and I end the call.

It's kind of fun. The phone rings again.

"Yes."

"Okay. We can make a deal." He's trying to remain calm. I don't speak.

"I'll take the two million for her."

I laugh. "But, you don't have her."

"You think you can just run off into the sunset a free man? You know he won't stop searching for you." I do know that. I'm not fucking stupid. I have no plans to run and hide.

"Your father has agreed to this?" He doesn't answer.

"I'll take that as a no. Unless I have his word too, I'm not making the deal." I hang up and place the phone on silent in my pocket. I pray to God that Kane says yes to the deal. I don't want to spend the rest of my life running.

They are in the sitting room that I interviewed Mary in. The moment I walk in, Maria's gaze pulls to me.

I hold her gaze until I sit beside her on the couch. She leans into me. It's slight, but I feel it.

"Where is Kane?" Larry asks and it's the first time I see fire in his brown eyes, eyes so similar to Maria's.

"It will be sorted," I say.

"I want to be there."

"Where, what's happening?" Maria looks at me.

"I'm going to meet Kane and King."

She's already shaking her head. "No. They will hurt you."

"I want them dead," Mary says holding her head high.

"Mum." Maria swings to Mary and her eyes fill with tears.

"You called me mum."

"You are my mother." Maria takes her hands and Mary breaks down again.

I look at Larry. "You can't come. But I promise it will end today."

"I said no." Maria is swinging back around.

The fear in her eyes, I want to remove, but I don't know how.

"They won't stop, Maria."

"Ring the police." She knows her suggestion isn't rational. "They kidnapped me." She looks to her father.

"It doesn't work like that." He answers her and it's the sad truth.

"Could I have a moment with Maria?" I hate to do this, but I need her to stay here.

"No." Mary surprises me when she holds Maria's hands. "She's not leaving my sight."

I don't look to Larry because I can't imagine he will be helpful. Maria doesn't lick her stubbornness up off the floor.

"A friend is coming with me."

"Which one?" Maria is looking at me and I see the warning in her eyes not to lie.

"Dean. You don't know him."

"What's going to happen?"

I glance at Larry and Mary, who are listening. It is their money that has funded this.

"Your parents gave me two million to get you back. So I used that money to pay a sniper."

I'm waiting for the outrage.

"How good is his shot?" Larry asks.

I smile. "He never misses."

Mary's hands tighten around Maria's hands. "Do what you need to do." I nod at her approval before I look at Maria.

Her eyes are swimming with worry.

"I'll be safe."

She swallows and shakes her head. "What if they hurt you? King killed Nate. Look at Charlie." She's shaking her head. "I can't let you go."

"We will never be safe if I don't do this." I want to take her hands but her mother is clinging to her and I won't dare try to pry her hands away. She looks like she'd kill me.

"You can't go."

"Maria," I say. She has to understand that we have no choice.

I don't know what she sees in my eyes but her lips start to tremble and it breaks my fucking heart. "No. Go back to the house and get Rome." Tears trickle down her face. If it's a lie she needs right now, it's a lie I'll give her.

"I'll get Rome."

She blinks and looks away from me. I don't delay. I see the pain in her eyes. I don't look back—because if I do—I fear I won't leave.

I stop by the house before meeting Kane and King. I have a message from King saying they want to meet me. I send them back the address. I have a bag filled with money, but I have no idea if this will go according to plan. After getting what I need out of the house, I take Rome from Jack.

"I have no idea when I'll be back, so you and Mattie can go home." I look back at the house. We will never return here.

"Jack. I need you to do one more thing for me."

"Anything."

"Can you check on Charlie? He's at the hospital. He's out of surgery, but he isn't responding."

"Yeah, I can do that."

Rome yips and I carry her to the car. She sniffs around the back seat. I keep the money in the front. My stomach twists. I would have never thought I would be in a situation like this.

I select the airplane strip, it's open and easy for Dean to set up on the roof. I have no idea if they will arrive. I'm the only car here at the hangar. I get out and walk around the area. I can see a car rolling up in the distance. I reach into the car and take out the bag of money.

I wait as Kane's car pulls up beside me. The piece in the back of my trousers feels heavy. I won't use it. I don't want to use it. I swore I would never spill blood again after killing the priests for William. I had gone to a place I swore I would never return to.

The door opens and my heart pounds. I have the urge to look up, but I don't want to give Dean's hiding place away.

Everything in me tenses as Kane's wife gets out. "Hello, Damien." I look behind her. She's alone. The bastard.

"She wasn't your target," I say, trying to stand straight.

"She was going to kill you." Dean stands over Rita. "Beautiful, right between the eyes."

I look at him. "King and Kane are the targets."

"No, the target was to be here and at this time. Are you really complaining?"

"No." I'm not. He saved my life. But I still have two more people that need to die.

"Nice doing business with you."

"You can't help me get her into the car?" I ask him. My side aches.

"I don't do the cleanup, sorry." He swings the rifle over his shoulder and leaves me with a dead body. I drag Rita to Kane's car and put her in the passenger side. Fear skitters across my skin as I worry that Kane and King are going after Maria. But they don't know where she is. Gathering up the money, I throw it into the back of my car. Rome yips and I roll down the window slightly before locking her in the vehicle. My side aches as I walk over to Kane's car. Removing the gun from my back pocket, I climb in. My eyes are drawn to Rita. Blood oozes from the bullet wound in-between her eyes. I place the gun beside her and it's like a mark on my soul. I don't want to use it.

I button up my shirt before driving back to Kane's. I want to turn around. I don't want to lose myself again by killing. As I approach his house, I promise myself that this is the last time. I drive into the driveway and someone is watching as the garage door opens. My stomach tightens. I reach across for the gun as I pull the car into the garage. I sit and wait. The door opens and King steps into the light. His face is pretty banged up. It must have been from Charlie.

"Ma." He squints into the car. I open the door and point the gun at him. His eyes grow wide.

"Where's my mother?" His fear grows.

"Passenger side," I tell him and point in the direction for him to move. He does while keeping his hands up. "Open it." I demand.

"You're making a mistake." His confident words have me keeping my back to the wall so I can watch the door. I know Kane is inside too.

"Open it." I repeat.

He does and there is such a moment of satisfaction when his mother's lifeless body tips over into his arms.

"That's what happens when you double cross me," I say.

He stands up and reaches for something. The gun is loud in the garage as he crumbles to the ground. I keep my eyes trained on the door as I walk around to King. It's a clean head shot. I wait beside the car for Kane to come, but he doesn't. Keeping the gun held high, I move to the door and listen.

"Kane." I call his name. No answer.

Stepping into the kitchen. It's empty.

I move from room to room and find him standing in his study. He isn't facing me and I look around the space.

"I never thought it would be you," he says turning to me. "Is my son dead?"

I nod and hold the gun up higher. His hands are in his pockets like he knew it would come to this.

"I can pay you." He half smiles.

I shake my head. "We are beyond that. Take your hands out of your pockets."

He does slowly and they are empty. "You shouldn't have forced my hand." I hate this. He deserved to die. He had to die.

"I underestimated you, Damien." He takes a step toward me. "Why are you hesitating?" There is a look of hope in his eyes. I have hesitated too long and maybe he believes that I won't do it.

"I'm not," I say and pull the trigger.

***

It has been three weeks since Maria was reunited with her parents. Three weeks of her mother hovering over her. She looks perfect as she stands beside her mother in a full-length red dress. She must feel my eyes on her as she glances over, before excusing herself. I can't look away as she sashays towards me.

I know how lucky I am. I'm aware of how everyone in the room gravitates towards my wife. "We need to go on more outings." She smiles when she reaches me.

"Why's that?" I lean in and inhale her while brushing a kiss on her red lips.

"You, in that suit." Her eyes grow darker.

My cock hardens. "We are in public." I remind her, but right now, I'd take her. "It's very hard to do anything with your mother watching."

Maria laughs and it's musical as she looks over at Mary who is watching her.

"She will relax soon. It's hard on her." Maria's eyes trail back to me.

"So beautiful and understanding." I brush another kiss on her lips. I've never seen anyone so strong.

"Tonight, when we get home…" She leaves the rest of her sentence open, but it's what I hold on to. I'll take her slowly and enjoy every inch of her flesh. That's the thought I hang onto as I brush another kiss against her lips.

"We might do it outside tonight," I whisper into her ear.

We're still staying with her parents. She'll never return to the other house and her mother isn't ready to let her move out, so for now, we are staying here.

"Why outside?" Maria doesn't look put off at all.

"So you can scream as loudly as you want."

She bites her lip. "We can leave early."

I smile. "We could take a walk around the castle. I can show you the areas that are off limits."

The charity function her parents are hosting is in Slane Castle, owned by Gerald. So I know I'll have access to all areas.

"I hear this place has some very naughty rooms." Maria takes my arm and I love the teasing tone.

"Who told you that?" I'm curious.

She taps her nose. "It doesn't matter. Is it true?"

I keep walking. "Why don't we find out?"

Her eyes are glowing with excitement and I glance back to see Mary still watching us. I nod at her and she nods back before turning back to the couple she was talking to. She knows I will keep Maria safe. I risked everything for her—my business, my life—and she's worth it.

At the O' Brien's residence, Maria also has the protection of Charlie, who is recovering. Tonight he's babysitting Rome, and a part of me believes that Charlie has found his place with us.

"So, are there like, orgies here?"

Maria's words snap me out of my thoughts and I stop walking. Tilting her chin up, I make her look at me.

"I will never, ever share you." I make it clear.

Her laugh is short as she leans into me and plants a kiss on my lips. "I will never share you, either."

Everything in me settles and I think for the first time, I've found peace.

THE END

I hope you enjoyed *Darker.*

Darkest is the next book in the Boyne Club Series.

Read Dean and Scarlett's story.

You can download HERE: https://author-vicarter.com/products/darker

Or scan the code below:

Or read on for a sneak peek:

DARKEST

CHAPTER ONE

Hunger can make us turn feral. Uncontrollable. I've made some pretty bad decisions while hungry. I've done things I'm not proud of for food. My stomach roars, and I tuck my chin into my chest as I walk down the main street. All's quiet at this time of the morning. A park beside the store has a few people jogging or out for an early morning walk. They look healthy and happy. *I hate them.* The warmth from the overhead heater blasts me as I enter the shop. The heat is enough to make me want to curl up under it and go to sleep. My bones ache like I'm eighty instead of twenty-one.

I stop, inhaling a deep breath. The scent of freshly made breakfast rolls wafts from the deli. My stomach gives another savage roar.

Don't linger, Scar. Just get what you need and get out.

My gaze roams over all the food. I want it all. I try to focus and not look so jumpy. Everything calls to me. My dirty sneakers shuffle forward and I'm standing in front of rows of colorful wrappers. My hands become clammy inside the wool gloves. The wool was once pink, now I can't really put a name to the color. Maybe grayish-pink.

My fingers wrap around the Mars Bar and my stomach roars again. It's too loud. A man glares at me. He doesn't look like an assistant; he looks like he owns the shop. He shakes his head slightly, telling me not to do it. My clothes tell the story of my homelessness. My long, unkempt hair is giving away my lack of money. I should put it back. Tears sting my eyes as I think of replacing the bar and going hungry.

It's a snap decision. My fingers tighten around the bar and I spin, tearing from the shop.

"Stop!"

I run faster and hit the door hard, nearly toppling over a woman pushing a pram. I want to apologize but the shop owner is right behind me. He lunges for me, but I skip away from his grasp and run out onto the road. A car horn beeps, making my heart race. The car screeches to a stop and I slam my hands on the bonnet. I meet the angry eyes of the driver before I continue running across the street.

"Come back!"

The shop owner is right behind me. *Oh, shit.* My feet hit last night's rainfall as I run down the alleyway. The moment I become aware of my surroundings, I know I'm caught. The alleyway cuts off—it's a dead end. A ladder attached to the building to my left hangs down close to the ground. I clutch my candy and race for it.

"Stop!" The shop owner's shouts make my thin legs move quicker. I grab the rung of the ladder and pull myself up. The rungs disappear under me as I scale the ladder quickly, and when I look down, he's glaring up at me with a promise in his eyes.

I fucked up. I know I did. My eyes water as I clear the ladder and roll onto the rooftop, landing on my back. My heart races a million miles an hour. I sit up and grip the brickwork and shuffle forward so I can peer back over the edge. He's no longer below me—he races back across the street. I don't take my focus off him until he turns and glares back up at the rooftop; I duck my head. I don't linger, but start to make my way across the building. A small wall separates the next roof. I cross the wall and grin. My stomach growls and I wrap my arms around my abdomen. I'm ready to sit down and start eating.

Everything in me stills as my vision zeroes in on a man lying flat on his stomach on the next rooftop over. I move forward, trying to get a better look at him. He's so still. He's dead. My stomach sours further.

Leave him, Scar.

My feet move quietly towards him. The saliva in my mouth dries up as I get closer. He's dead. Oh, God. I need to tell someone. Why is he up here? Maybe to sleep? There are a lot of homeless people in Dublin, far more than there should be. I chew my cracked and dry lips until a metallic taste fills my mouth. I stop moving as my gaze hones in on a long black rifle that's lying against his shoulder. Fear shoots through me as I continue to study the man. His head moves ever so slightly, his eye against the scope. The movement causes my heart to skyrocket and fear buzzes and rattles in my bones. I need to leave. He's not dead. I need to leave now.

The rifle aims out towards the park. Bile crawls up my throat.

Go, Scar.

A man jogs in the park. He's oblivious to the shooter who has trained his rifle on him. The shooter shifts slightly, rolling his shoulder as he moves his finger to the trigger.

He pulls the trigger.

The click is soft, but it's like a punch to my stomach as the jogger falls to the ground. People around him stop, and a woman starts to scream. More people come over with hesitation in their steps to see why she is screaming. There's a lot of commotion and crimson liquid leaves the jogger's head.

I swallow more bile. The shooter's dark eyes connect with me and I'm ready to throw up. The rooftop disappears quickly as I run for my life. I know he's chasing me from the shift in the space behind me. He isn't making much noise but he's there. I won't look back, I want to so badly but I need to focus. I clear another wall and jump. I have no idea what I will land on. I hit the surface and feel a burning in my ankle, but I don't slow down. The heavy thud has me looking back. He's cleared the wall. His eyes are filled with violence that he will unleash on me if I get caught. I jump from one building to the next. The gap is small but my body hits the new rooftop hard. It knocks the air from my lungs. I scramble back up and fall sideways, my body giving up on me. A hand grabs my shoulder and spins me mid-fall. I tumble to the ground and I'm staring into the barrel of a gun.

My hand moves slowly into my pocket, where I left my bar. I can't let it go. I can't lose it. It's stupid that I'm thinking about the food when I'm about to die. But in case I somehow survive this, I'll have food.

"What are you doing up here, little girl?"

Little girl? I take another look at the man, but my fear makes everything buzzy and fuzzy.

The tip of the rifle is cold as he presses it against my cheek. "Answer the fucking question."

"I was hiding."

His eyes dart to my pocket that I still have my hand in. "What's in your pocket?"

I'm shaking my head. He can't have my candy. I'll starve. My logic has left me and I can't reason with the madness right now.

"Take your hand out of your pocket slowly, or I'll pull the trigger."

The hairs rise on the back of my neck. My heart is ready to leap from my body and nose-dive off the side of the building. Maybe running and jumping would be better than being shot up here. How long would it take for anyone to find me? I have no one who would look for me. Would anybody care? I look longingly at the edge.

The man cocks the gun and my attention is drawn back to him. As I slowly remove my hand from my pocket, he moves back slightly, but I can see in his eyes that he is ready to pull the trigger. My vision wavers as I slowly hold out the Mars Bar. His gun points at the candy. I blink and tears spill as I open my fingers. The bar is squashed. I'm sure it's also melted from the sweat that soaks my hand. I'll still eat it if I live long enough.

A half cry bubbles from my lips. The man's dark eyes focus on my face.

"Who are you hiding from, little girl?" He holds the gun to my head again.

Tiredness rattles my bones and I let my eyelids flutter closed. I tighten my hold on my prize. "The shopkeeper."

"Open your eyes." The barrel of the rifle presses into my cheek. The cold steel has me alert and my heart starts a new rhythm of fear.

"I saw nothing," I plead, not ready to die.

"You stole that bar?" His eyes go to my candy and I pull it close to my chest. My stomach roars again. I just want to eat it. I think of asking him if

I can have the bar before he pulls the trigger. Let me die with something in my stomach.

"Can I eat it?" I ask.

His eyes darken. Half his face is covered in black hair. His beard is thick and I wonder if food ever gets stuck in all that hair.

He takes a step closer and my eyelids squeeze together. This is it. Not how I expected my life to end. I thought I would starve to death in an alleyway or be mugged for my pitiful belongings. My hand reaches for my neck where the one and only possession I have hangs. I don't get to touch, I don't get to run my fingers across the pendant one more time.

Pain explodes behind my lids and burns my face. My stomach roils and the world tilts as I hit the ground. I can't see. My skull is on fire. Is this what death is? No images flash before my eyes. I blink and the last thing I see is large military boots before the world drags me to the pit of hell.

Download and read HERE: https://author-vicarter.com/products/darker
Or scan the code below:

OTHER BOOKS BY VI CARTER

THE CELLS OF KALASHOV

THE COLLECTOR #1

THE SIXTH #2

THE HANDLER #3

MURPHY'S MAFIA MADE MEN

SINNER'S VOW #1

SAVAGE MARRIAGE #2

SCANDALOUS PLEDGE #3

SONS OF THE MAFIA

SINS OF THE MAFIA #0.5

VENGEANCE IN BLOOD #1

YOUNG IRISH REBELS SERIES

MAFIA PRINCE #1

MAFIA KING #2

MAFIA GAMES #3

MAFIA BOSS #4

MAFIA SECRETS #5 (NOVELLA)

WILD IRISH SERIES

FATHER (PREQUEL)

VICIOUS #1

RECKLESS #2

RUTHLESS #3

FEARLESS #4

HEARTLESS #5

THE BOYNE CLUB

DARK #1

DARKER # 2

DARKEST #3

PITCH BLACK #4

THE OBSESSED DUET

A DEADLY OBSESSION #1

A CRUEL CONFESSION #2

BROKEN PEOPLE DUET

BREAK ME #1

SAVE ME #2

ABOUT THE AUTHOR

A bout the Author

Vi Carter - the queen of **DARK ROMANCE**, the mistress of suspense, and the high priestess of *PLOT TWISTS*!

When she's not busy crafting tales of the **MAFIA** that'll leave you on the edge of your seat, you can find her baking up a storm, exploring the gorgeous Irish countryside, or spending time with her three little girls.

Vi's Young Irish Rebels series has been praised by readers and can be found in English, Dutch, German, Audible and soon will be available in French.

And let's not forget her two greatest loves: ***coffee and chocolate***. If you ever need to bribe her, just offer up a mug of coffee and a slab of chocolate, and she'll be putty in your hands.

So, if you're ready to join Vi on a wild journey with the mafia, sign up for her newsletter and score a free book! Just be warned - her stories are so **ADDICTIVE**, you might not be able to put them down.

What Readers Are Saying

Editorial Reviews

"Vi Carter has once again blown my mind with another outstanding story. She never fails to create a masterpiece with memorable characters that leap off the page. This book is complete perfection."- USA Today Bestselling Author Khardine Gray

Vi is one of those authors who never disappoints. She weaves **LOVE** & **DANGER** effortlessly. ★★★★★ stars

I definitely recommend this book. It is **SUSPENSEFUL** and exciting. I enjoy reading Vi Carter's book. ★★★★★ stars

How to Keep in Touch with Vi Carter

Visit Vi's website: https://author-vicarter.com/
Join the newsletter: t.ly/yZWbX
Or scan the code below:

On Facebook, Instagram, TikTok and YouTube @darkauthorvicarter and on Twitter @authorvicarter
Or scan the code below:

9 781915 878588